JESSICA BECK

THE DONUT MYSTERIES, BOOK 38
PERJURY PROOF

Disclaimer:
For the purposes of this book, the poison vanalaxis macromium is entirely fictional. The last thing this author wants to do is write a How-To manual on murder, so be advised that this fictional household cleaner is merely part of a larger piece of fiction created solely for your enjoyment.

The First Time Ever Published!

The 38th Donut Mystery.

Jessica Beck is the *New York Times* Bestselling Author of the
Donut Mysteries, the Classic Diner Mysteries, the Ghost
Cat Cozy Mysteries, and the Cast Iron Cooking Mysteries.

This one's for Auriel,
A true princess in all of the very best ways.
You may be gone,
but you will live on in the hearts of those
of us who loved you forever.

A pie shop is opening up in April Springs, but the owner is as sour as her pies are sweet! When she's murdered a few days before the grand opening, too many folks in April Springs had reasons to want to see the woman gone. Suzanne and Grace dive into the case, hopefully in time to save the next victim on the killer's to-do list!

CHAPTER 1

I've been a sucker for freshly baked pies since I was a little girl, so when I heard that Sky High Pie was going to open in our little town of April Springs, North Carolina, I was the first to celebrate the news.

But then I met the new owner, Maggie Moore—as bitter as a sour cherry and as puny in spirit as a crabapple—so I wasn't exactly shocked by what happened next, though I had no idea at the time how much pain and suffering my investigation of her murder would cause me.

"Do you have a problem with me, young lady?" the stranger demanded fiercely as she stormed into my donut shop one bright autumn day and confronted me without so much as a how-do-you-do. Fall was my favorite season of year—well, at least one of the top four—and I'd been in a good mood up until a few seconds ago.

"No. Why, should I?"

"I'm sorry. You'll have to speak up. I'm a little hard of hearing." The woman's face seemed to have a permanent scowl imprinted on it. Somewhere in her late fifties, my bad-mannered visitor was pudgy, but not in a cute way. Her hair, dappled with gray, looked tired, and her clothes were loose and flowing, as though she was trying to hide her bulk under yards and yards of pretty unimpressive fabric.

"Why would I have a problem with you? I don't even know you," I said, raising my voice well above my normal comfort level. It managed to get the attention of some of my customers, who looked at me oddly for a moment before going back to their meals. Did they actually think that I was shouting at this woman on purpose?

"Well, you don't have to scream," she said, chastising me. "Lower your voice a bit."

"Sorry," I said as I searched for a volume she could hear, but not loud enough to drive off my regular customers. "Who are you?"

"I'm Maggie Moore," she said. "Gabby Williams is my cousin."

That explained some of her behavior if the two women were cut from the same cloth. Gabby and I had an odd relationship that could best be described as a confrontational friendship, if that made any sense at all.

"And Gabby told you that I had a problem with you?" I asked her, feeling a little surreal even having this conversation with a total stranger.

"She said you didn't like competition," Maggie replied fiercely.

"Do you make donuts, too?" I asked, not having a clue as to exactly where this conversation was going.

"What? You'll have to speak up. I already told you that."

"Are you a donut maker?" I asked her a little louder than I'd intended.

"Pies," she said, dropping her lower lip, as though the idea of making donuts for a living was clearly beneath her. "We make pies."

"You're the new pie shop owner?" I asked. I'd been meaning to visit her shop before she held her grand opening in a few days, but I'd had my hands full running Donut Hearts solo. Emma had been gone for a few weeks on a trip with her mother, Sharon,

2

and I'd been running the shop alone. Those Blake women loved to travel, though Ray, Emma's father and Sharon's husband, was a real homebody, so he rarely joined them on their excursions.

"I am. So, is it true? Do you have an issue with me opening a shop of my own in April Springs?" This woman was downright belligerent. I didn't care if she made the best pies known to man, if she didn't figure out a way to deal with her customers, as well as her fellow small business owners, she'd go broke in six months. After all, I knew better than most that there was more to running a shop than offering delightful goods.

"I'm happy to have you in April Springs," I said loudly, deciding to just ignore her foul temper and accusatory tones. "When exactly is your grand opening? I'll shut down my shop early to be there." I had been looking forward to the place opening ever since I heard that she'd be coming to town, and I wasn't going to let her off-putting demeanor keep me away, at least not initially.

"We're having a soft opening tomorrow," she said. "You can come and have a look around. Bring your husband with you."

"I'd love to, but he's out of town at the moment," I explained.

"What did you just say? He's out of his mind?"

This woman was driving me crazy! "He's away on business," I said louder.

She nodded, frowning at the same time. "Oh. Well then, good-bye."

"While you're here, would you like a donut?" I offered.

Maggie Moore looked at my display cases for a few moments, and then she frowned at me again. "How much are they?"

"I'd love one to be my gift to you as a way of welcoming you to our community," I said.

"Okay. I'll take a dozen on the house, since you're offering," she said with a nod. "Mix them up. Your call."

Had the blasted woman purposefully misheard my offer

of one donut and demanded a dozen? It was near enough to closing time, and unfortunately I had the inventory to spare, so I decided to be the bigger woman, though *she* was clearly the bigger woman, at least when it came to getting on the scales. It was a cheap shot, but I didn't care. I was a little on the heavy side myself, given my line of work, but that hadn't made *me* grumpy.

"Of course," I said as I got her a dozen of my least popular selections.

As I handed the box to her, she asked, "Where's my free coffee?"

"Sorry, we're fresh out," I said. It was true in a way, since we were completely out of *free* coffee. If she wanted something to drink, she was going to have to pay for it, at least if she was getting it from me.

The news seemed to disappoint her even further as she collected her donuts and left without even as much as thanking me.

Wow, that woman was going to be hard to live with.

Her pies had better be out of this world.

"What was that all about?" Paige Hill asked as she approached my counter a few seconds later.

"Did you hear that?" I asked the bookshop owner as I refreshed her coffee.

"How could I not?" Paige asked, shaking her head in disbelief. She'd gotten in the habit of joining me for a quick break whenever her schedule allowed it, and I loved her company. Paige was my kind of storeowner, a real credit to the April Springs downtown business district. Well, I suppose it was a little ambitious calling us that, since our "group" was comprised of just a handful of stores and shops. "She's as deaf as a post, isn't she?"

"And as mean as a snake, too," I said. "That wasn't just me, was it? She really wasn't very pleasant, was she?"

"I can't believe you didn't throw her out on the spot. If she comes by the bookstore looking for free samples, she's going to find her way out the back door in a heartbeat."

I looked out the window and saw that Maggie was indeed heading straight for The Last Page bookshop. "Don't look now, but I believe you're getting a visitor."

"Blast it all," Paige said as she headed straight for the door, leaving her coffee undrunk. "Bye."

"Don't forget to speak up," I said with a grin.

Paige shook her head as she raced out, and I saw her catch Maggie on the sidewalk before she could go inside. The two of them had a conversation right out in front of the bookstore, and it appeared to go even more poorly than mine had. To make matters worse, I saw Gabby Williams approaching the two women, no doubt to show support for her cousin. I wasn't about to let Paige get ambushed alone, so I looked over at my last two customers and said, "I'll be right back. Help yourself to coffee refills."

"And more donuts, too?" Seth Lancaster asked with a grin.

"Sure, just leave your money on the counter and take whatever you'd like," I replied.

Seth shrugged as I was leaving, but I knew that I could trust him. The man was a bit prickly on the outside at times, but he'd developed a soft spot for his grandchildren, and it had made the old guy somehow human, a testament to the amazing transformative power of love.

Gabby Williams, the stylish and trim owner of ReNEWed—a gently used elegant clothing shop located right next to mine— was just joining the fray when I got onto the scene.

"Paige Hill, are you standing out in front of everyone in town and yelling at my cousin?" Gabby asked fiercely. That would have been a neat trick in and of itself, since only the four of us were out there at the time.

"You have to yell at her in order to be heard," I said from behind Gabby. My presence caught her off guard as she twirled to look at me.

"Don't you start with me, Suzanne Hart."

"Gabby, I don't need *you* to fight my battles for me," Maggie said fiercely to her cousin. "I'm perfectly capable of handling the likes of these two by myself."

"I'm just trying to help," Gabby said, clearly exasperated by being confronted on two fronts. Paige was looking on at the moment, clearly bemused by the situation now that we'd stepped in.

"I can handle myself," Maggie answered, much louder than was necessary.

Gabby frowned at each of us in turn, and then she turned and headed back to her shop without another word. I'd have to mend that fence later, but for now, I needed Paige to know that I had her back. Once Gabby was gone, Maggie turned away as well, but as she did, I saw her let the box of my donuts "accidentally" slip from her grip, spilling the contents onto the ground.

"Whoops," she said with clear delight—the first time I'd seen her actually smile—and then she left us without making the least effort to clean up the mess she'd just made of my delightful treats.

I knelt down to pick up the remnants of the donuts and jam them back into the box, with Paige pitching in as well.

"I'm so sorry, Suzanne. This is awful."

"No worries. I was going to have to pitch them out soon anyway," I said as I got most of a blueberry-stuffed donut back into the box. My hand was going to be stained with all kinds of different fillings, and the whole thing just made me sad. It was like some kind of gruesome donut homicidal rampage.

"It's just not right," she said, grabbing a Boston cream donut and trying to get most of it back into the box as well. At least that filling wouldn't stain her hands. "That woman is impossible."

"She can't even get along with her own cousin," I said, feeling a little better having Paige commiserate with me. "What hope did we have?"

"Well, I for one am going to boycott her pie shop when she opens it tomorrow," Paige said.

"I don't know. Maybe we should give her *one* more chance," I replied.

Paige looked at me for a moment before breaking out into a grin. "I suppose it's the neighborly thing to do, isn't it?"

"Maybe there will be free samples," I said, laughing outright now.

"There had better be," Paige answered as we finished cleaning up the sidewalk in front of her shop as best as we could. "Don't worry about the rest of it. I'll rinse the walkway with a few buckets of water, and no one will ever know what happened."

"I don't know about you, but I doubt that *I'll* be able to forget," I said.

As I was leaving, Paige called out, "By the way, thanks for coming to my rescue earlier."

"I wasn't about to let the two of them gang up on you," I replied. "You would have done the same thing for me."

"You'd better believe I would have," she answered.

Seth was waiting for me by the front door, and he held it open for me as I got back to Donut Hearts. "That woman should be shot for slaughtering your donuts like that," he said.

"Did you see what happened?" I asked him. I hadn't even realized that anyone else had been watching.

"I did, and I'm not the only one, either. Do you want me to go talk to her, Suzanne?"

This was new. Since when did Seth Lancaster stick up for me? "No, I'm good, but thanks for the offer."

"You bet," he said, and then he left my shop, clearly still fuming about what had happened outside.

I wasn't all that pleased myself.

If Maggie Moore was looking to start something with me, I was bound and determined to finish it, and I had a hunch that I wasn't alone in my animosity for the pie maker. What a shame. Someone who should have been my natural ally was very possibly going to be one of my biggest foes.

CHAPTER 2

A FTER CLOSING UP DONUT HEARTS for the day, I couldn't seem to get Maggie Moore off of my mind. I suppose I'm like most folks. I want *everyone* to like me when it comes down to it, and Maggie's off-putting behavior had been bothering me since I'd met her. I finished cleaning up the shop and balancing out my register, and then, after dropping my meager earnings off at the bank, I decided to take the last eleven donuts I'd had in unsold inventory to Maggie. Maybe I'd just caught her having a bad moment. After all, I knew the stress involved in opening a food shop in April Springs more than just about anyone else around.

I drove over to the location of Maggie's shop, just off Viewmont Avenue between the town clock and the Episcopal Church. She was across the road from the town hall and the police station, near the building I had inherited from my father as well, and I had a hunch she'd have no shortage of customers if her pies were any good at all.

The front door of the building was locked, which didn't surprise me. I knocked a few times anyway, but no one answered. For a second I thought about just leaving the donuts with a note, but I knew in my heart that was taking the coward's way out. I needed to see the woman face to face to see if we could at least come to some kind of mutual respect. After all, that's what I'd done with Gabby Williams, and now, much to my astonishment, we'd actually become friends, in a loose definition of the word.

Maybe her cousin wouldn't be all that different if I just made a bit of an effort.

As I knocked on the back door, it opened almost immediately upon my touch. Had it not even been closed completely? "Hello?" I called out as I started to edge through the door when someone suddenly appeared, blocking my way as well as my view.

It wasn't Maggie, though.

"May I help you?" a young woman in her late teens or early twenties asked, clearly frazzled by something. She absently fussed with her hair, mostly pulled back but with strands of wispy blonde coming through, and she pushed a little of the mop back off her forehead, adding another smudge of flour to the one already there.

"I'm Suzanne Hart," I said. "I'd love to speak with Maggie."

"Sorry, she's not here at the moment. At least I don't think so. She's been coming in and out all day, and I've been too busy to notice. After all, these pies aren't going to make themselves," the young woman said after a quick glance back into the shop. Was she lying to me? I had to wonder if Maggie had sent her out to deal with me so she wouldn't have to.

"Could you check and see if she's here? If so, I have a gift for her, but if not, do you have any idea where she might have gone?" I asked as I tried my best to peek around the door. This young woman's forehead wasn't the only thing dappled with flour. There was a great deal of it on the floor of the kitchen as well, along with footprints going back and forth in it, tracking the place up like a winter wonderland scene in a picture book.

"I wish I could drop everything and track her down, but things are kind of crazy right now," she said after glancing back inside again ever so briefly. Was this poor child so overwhelmed that she was about to have a nervous breakdown, even at her young age?

It was clear I wasn't going to get the audience I'd been hoping for, but that didn't mean that I had to go away without at least making some kind of effort.

"You must be new in town," I told her with my brightest smile. "I've told you my name. What's yours?"

She did her best to smile under what appeared to be trying circumstances, which I was sure they were, given the fact that she'd chosen to work with Maggie Moore. "I'm Leanne Haller," she said as she offered me a floured hand.

I took it and found that a firm handshake went along with her attempted smile. "It's nice to meet you, Leanne. I'm assuming you are here working for Maggie?"

"Yes. As a matter of fact, Maggie is my aunt," Leanne said, though it was clear the information gave her no great joy to share.

"So you must be related to Gabby Williams, too," I answered.

"No, I'm from the *other* side of the family. I suppose we're related somehow, but not by blood." It was an odd distinction to make, I thought.

"How are you enjoying your time in April Springs so far?" I asked, hoping to get something out of this young woman.

"Honestly, I haven't seen much of it since I arrived two weeks ago. My aunt has been keeping me busy in the kitchen experimenting with the pies while she handles the business end of things."

That news surprised me for some reason. "So then, *you're* the pie maker?"

"Yes, I've been baking since I could walk, practically. Aunt Maggie decided to open the business, so she hired me to make the pies."

That seemed a bit like the tail wagging the dog to me. "Are

you at least equal partners in the business?" I asked her. I knew that it was none of my concern, but somehow it felt as though Maggie was exploiting her niece's talents if all she brought to the table was the business end of things. I knew how important that aspect was, but without a pie maker, there really wasn't any business at all.

"No, but maybe I will be someday. Right now, I'm happy enough just being an employee here," she said. Her eyes lit up as she asked, pointing to the box in my hands, "Are those the town donuts I've been hearing so many good things about?"

"I certainly hope so. I own Donut Hearts, and I made these myself," I said as I offered her the box.

Leanne forgot me for a moment as she opened the box and peered inside. "Is that Boston cream?" she asked. Before I could answer, she took a bite of it, and then smiled. There was nothing timid about her joy in that taste. "That filling is not from a box or a bag, is it?"

"No, I make most of the fillings myself," I admitted. Not many folks had that educated a palate, but it mattered to me that my donuts were as fresh and as homemade as I could manage.

"It's really excellent," she said, and then she frowned for a moment.

"Is something wrong, Leanne?"

"Maybe there's something you could help me with, baker to baker. I'm having a little trouble with my custard tarts at the moment. Would you try one and tell me what you think?" She was clearly in a tailspin about it.

"I'm not sure if I can help, but I'm certainly willing to try."

"Excellent," she said, and then, to my surprise, she shut the door in my face.

What an odd young woman! I thought about knocking after twenty seconds, but the door suddenly sprang open again. "I'm sorry about that, but Maggie doesn't allow anyone else inside, and frankly, it's not worth the scolding I would get if she caught you in here," she said as she thrust a tart upon me. "There's just something not right about it, but I can't put my finger on it."

The crust was superb, so I knew that wasn't the problem. After taking a small bite of the tart, I tried to discern why she was unhappy with it. I agreed, something was not quite perfect, but it was close. "How much lemon zest did you use?"

"Half a strip," she said. "I was afraid to use much more. I didn't want to overpower it. After all, it's not a lemon tart."

"No, but there needs to be more than just a hint. If you use an entire strip of zest, and maybe even a smidge more, it may add that undertone you expect from a good tart." The reason I could converse so fluently about tarts was because my husband had gone through a phase six months earlier when he'd pled with me to make them. One of the protagonists from a BBC show favored them above all else, and Jake had rued the fact that he couldn't get fresh custard tarts in our part of North Carolina. I'd taken it as a challenge, and after dragooning my mother into my mission, we'd made tart after tart until we were both satisfied with the results. Jake had been over the moon about them, but after a few months, he'd decided that he'd rather have one of my mother's pies after all, so we'd dropped our tart making.

"You're right. How could I not see that?" she asked.

"Don't be so hard on yourself. They are still very good right now."

"Good isn't good enough, at least according to my aunt," she said with a wry smile. I was beginning to like this young lady. "Thanks for the advice, and the donuts."

Leanne started to close the door on me when I managed to stop its movement just in time. "I would be happy to help more, if you'd like. My husband's out of town, so I've got loads of time on my hands at the moment." Jake was still away guarding a CEO in Virginia, a job that had started out to be just two weeks but was now heading into its third month. I'd seen him a time or two since, but ever so briefly. He assured me that he'd be wrapping things up soon, but I'd heard that before. Still, he was happy tracking down the man making threats against his employer, that much I could tell, so I hadn't pushed it.

"As much as I would love to take you up on that, I'm afraid that Aunt Maggie would never allow it," Leanne said ruefully as she pushed the door firmly closed.

What a curious young woman. She was clearly adept in the kitchen if that tart was any sampling, but I hated the way her aunt had managed to intimidate her. It gave me just one more reason not to like Maggie Moore, not that I'd needed one.

And then I heard a hard voice from behind me, saying "Suzanne" in a way that made it sound more like a curse than a name.

I knew that voice too well to even have to turn around to identify the speaker. "Hi, Gabby."

"What are you doing here?" she asked me critically.

So much for pleasantries, then. "I wanted to see if I could smooth things over with your cousin. I'm afraid we got off to a rather rocky start."

That seemed to mollify Gabby some, but she still wasn't totally at ease. "You didn't even bring a peace offering?"

"As a matter of fact, I brought donuts, but Maggie wouldn't or couldn't see me. I suspect she's hiding somewhere in the back, but I met Leanne. She seemed really nice."

Gabby frowned at that news. "That's odd."

"Why, don't you *like* Leanne?" I asked her, deliberately misunderstanding her point. After all, she'd started in on me from the beginning of this conversation, and I wasn't about to take it easy on her.

"Leanne is fine. We're not related by blood, you know," Gabby said.

"Why is that so important to everyone? She mentioned it herself."

"Let's just say there are some hard feelings between my side of the family and hers. It dates back to nearly a hundred years ago when one of our great-grandfathers was accused of stealing from the other one." Gabby frowned for a second before adding, "No matter what, she's still a Haller, even if we *are* related."

"Let me get this straight. You all *still* have a problem with each other after nearly a hundred years? That's a little long to hold a grudge, isn't it?"

"There's no way you can understand," Gabby said dismissively. She brushed past me and knocked on the door with three sharp raps.

There was no answer at all this time.

Gabby got close to the door and practically shouted, "Maggie! Leanne! It's Gabby! Open up and let me in!"

There was still no reply.

"Maybe they are tied up," I said, trying my best not to smile. After all, at least Leanne had answered my summons, even if she hadn't let me in.

"Nonsense," Gabby said. It was clear that she wasn't about to be thwarted. As she pounded on the door again, I was fearful that it wouldn't be able to withstand the blows. I also worried about Gabby's hand. How much more punishment could it take?

Then, to my surprise, I heard a police car's siren and saw flashing lights as a squad car tore out from the parking lot across the street and screeched to a halt in the back of the pie shop building where we stood.

"What's going on, Chief?" I asked Chief Grant as he raced out of his cruiser. He and my best friend, Grace, were in the final stages of breaking up, or so it looked to me, and that had cooled our relationship as well. I was a big fan of the chief per se, but Grace was more than like a sister to me; we were more a part of each other's lives than many true siblings I knew.

"Step aside," the chief said dismissively.

"I demand answers," Gabby said, refusing to do as he instructed.

"Gabby, don't push me right now," he said, and then he banged on the door twice.

"That won't do you any good," Gabby crowed, but then, to our surprise, the door opened and a very shaken Leanne appeared.

"Where is she?" the chief asked.

"Back here," Leanne stammered before starting to collapse. It was interesting to note that she moved to me for support, and not Gabby.

As the chief disappeared inside, I asked Leanne, "Are you okay?"

"Yes. No. I don't know." It was clear the poor girl was in a state of shock.

"What happened, Leanne?" Gabby asked, her voice rattling the wind as she spoke.

"It's Maggie. She's dead."

"What do you mean, she's dead?" Gabby asked her critically.

"I found her in her office with one of my tarts still in her hand," Leanne said. Her entire body shook as she spoke, and I wondered how she was ever going to live with herself if her treat had killed her aunt. I'd been accused of something like that myself in the past, but thankfully I'd been exonerated, though not without a great deal of detective work on my part.

"Is that what *killed* her?" Gabby asked, studying her with the most ominous glare I'd ever seen in my life.

"No! Of course not! It must have been the pills," she said.

"What pills?" Gabby asked.

"For her heart. They were scattered everywhere."

I had to see this for myself. "Will you be okay?" I asked her.

"Yes. I think so," she muttered.

"I'll be right back," I said, and then I started inside after the chief of police.

"Where do you think you are going, Suzanne Hart?" Gabby asked me accusingly.

"I'm going to see what's going on for myself," I said.

When I found the chief, he was studying Maggie's body, which was still seated in her chair behind her desk, slumped over. Her face was hard to see since her head was lying on the desktop, but it was unmistakably her. From what I could see, there was nothing peaceful about the way she'd died, and I could smell death in the air.

The chief of police took a few quick photos with his phone, and I wanted to do the same thing, but I didn't think that would be acceptable to him. He shook his head in disgust as our gazes met. "How can someone do this to themselves?" he asked as he gestured toward the spilled pills and the empty bottle on the desktop. I spied the tart, identical to the one I'd tasted earlier, still clutched in one of her hands, squeezed nearly beyond recognition. Had she taken a bite to make the pills a little more palatable going down?

"Is she really dead?" I asked.

"Yes, she's cool to the touch. I don't know how long it took for that girl to find her, but by the time she did, it was too late."

"Would you say she's been dead for longer than twenty minutes, or less than that?" I asked him.

"I'd say longer, though I'll need the coroner's report to be sure," he said. "Why? When was the last time *you* saw her?" Then he twigged to something he must have seen coming in. "You brought her donuts. I saw them on my way in."

"Twice, as a matter of fact. Well, I gave her the first ones myself, but she accidentally dropped them in front of The Last Page, so I decided to replace them." There was no reason to speak ill of the dead at that point, so I kept our little spat to myself. After all, I didn't see how that could contribute to her killing herself. I'd had a friend in college who had suffered from depression, so I knew how serious it could be, but Shandra had been a sensitive soul. Every sling and arrow from the world seemed to impact her. I knew that illness could take many forms, but Maggie hadn't struck me as someone who would let anything get through her tough-as-nails demeanor. Then again, do we really ever know anyone else, especially after one brief meeting? For all I knew, she'd been struggling with depression for years until she finally succumbed to it.

"Well, at least it appears that you are in the clear on this one," the chief said.

I hadn't even considered myself *out* of the clear! "What happens now?" I asked him.

"We still have to do an autopsy," he said. "I'll have my crew take photos and video as a matter of procedure, but this looks like a clear case of suicide to me." The police chief frowned for a second, and then he studied me a moment or two before speaking. "How's Grace doing?"

"I wouldn't even begin to know how to answer that," I said a little curtly. He knew whose side I was on.

"Yeah. Sure. Okay." We both looked up as we heard EMTs coming through the door. "Suzanne, you need to go."

"Sure thing," I said. I had no desire to be around a dead body anyway, especially if she'd taken her own life. Frankly, I'd been amazed the chief of police hadn't thrown me out immediately. He must be in some real pain himself, but I couldn't let myself dwell on that. Grace needed me. After all, Chief Grant had his own friends, including my husband and the mayor, though neither man was in town at the moment. Jake was away for work, while the mayor was taking a little time off after the murder of someone very close to him. I was sorry if that put Chief Grant in a bad place, but there was really nothing I could do about that. Gals before pals, after all, and even though Stephen Grant and I were friends, Grace was a part of me.

"How bad is it?" Gabby asked me as I emerged from the building. I saw that she was now supporting Leanne, although she looked entirely uncomfortable doing it.

I just shook my head and turned toward her niece. "Leanne, when was the last time you saw her? Do you recall?"

"It was quite a bit before you brought us donuts. Remember, I didn't even know if she was in the building or not when you asked about her. When I'm baking, I tend to lose all track of time," she said quickly. "Maggie tried one of my first batches of tarts, though that feels as though it was hours ago."

"What did she think of it?" I asked.

"Suzanne, that's hardly relevant now," Gabby said, scolding me as always, which seemed to be her fallback position.

"She said that she thought it was fine, but she really didn't have a very good sense of taste. It was nearly as bad as her hearing," Leanne said softly.

"And yet she wanted to open a pie shop, something that taste is critical for if it is going to have any chance of succeeding," I said, marveling yet again how some people choose the businesses they run.

"That's why she had me," Leanne said as she continued to stare at the door and started to waver again. I had a hunch she was in shock, and the enormity of what she'd found was just beginning to sink in. I knew I needed to get her out of there, and fast. Her aunt's body was going to be leaving on a gurney soon enough, and the poor girl didn't need to go through that.

"Is there anyone in town who can take care of you?" I asked, getting ready to invite her back to my cottage if there wasn't. After all, there was plenty of room there. She could have the entire upstairs, including my old bedroom and bath. Honestly, it might be nice having a bit of company.

"That won't be necessary. She's coming with me," Gabby said as she put a protective arm around her niece.

My eyebrows must have shot up. I wanted to ask her if that was in spite of the feud, but Gabby didn't stick around to hear my clever retorts. "I'll see you later," I told Leanne gently as Gabby led her away. "Hang in there."

"I'll try. Thanks for being here for me," she said.

"You bet," I answered.

There was no reason for me to stick around the pie shop once they were both gone. I didn't have any need to see Maggie's dead body being wheeled out, especially if it hadn't been murder. The chief had acted oddly when he'd asked about my best friend, so I decided to see if I could find Grace and see what exactly was going on with the two of them.

CHAPTER 3

"I WAS JUST GOING TO LEAVE you a note to tell you to come see me," I told Grace when she answered the door in her bathrobe, her hair put up in a towel. I knew that her working hours were mostly her own in her job as a cosmetic company's sales supervisor, subject to the whims of whoever her current boss might be, at any rate.

"Now you don't have to," she said. "I decided to take a mental health day. Well, an afternoon, at any rate. How goes the world of donuts?"

"You haven't heard the news, have you?" I asked her as I stepped inside her neat and stylish home. She'd been raised there, just a few hundred feet down the road from me, and when her parents had passed away, it had become hers.

"What news is that? I just got home, thus my current state of undress."

"Maggie Moore killed herself an hour ago," I said, guessing about the time.

"That's terrible," Grace said, slumping back a little against the doorframe. "Who exactly is Maggie Moore? Or was, I suppose I should say."

"She was the woman who was all set to open the pie shop," I said. "We had an argument earlier this morning, and I was trying to take her some donuts to make peace with her when her niece found the body. Her name is Leanne, and she was working for Maggie."

"That is truly tragic," Grace said. "April Springs is kind of an odd place to decide to open a pie shop in the first place, isn't it? I mean we have your donuts, and the grocery store has a bakery, even if our town bakery shut down last year, which might be considered an omen in and of itself. It seems a little like overkill, if you ask me." She blanched slightly at her word choice. "You know what I mean."

"She was Gabby Williams's cousin, which might explain why she came here," I explained.

"So that would make her related to Leanne as well," Grace said.

"Yes, but not by blood," I amended automatically.

My best friend looked at me quizzically for a moment before speaking. "Is that really relevant, Suzanne?"

"I didn't think so before today, but evidently it's a real sticking point with *this* family. There's some story about bad blood between the great-grandfathers, but I didn't get the whole story."

"I don't see how that could possibly matter at this point." Grace's expression softened a little. "Suzanne, you don't feel responsible for that woman killing herself just because you two had an argument, do you?"

"Of course not," I said. "I just wanted you to know why it bothered me so much."

"So, I guess there isn't going to be a pie shop in town after all," Grace said.

"I'm not so sure about that. Leanne is the piemaker. Maggie was just the business end of the operation. Maybe Momma will want to take her on as a pet project until she gets on her feet." My mother had been known to step into failing businesses to help right them in the past. She was fond of April Springs in a way that I couldn't match, often putting her money where her mouth was behind the scenes. Usually Momma's only caveat to the people she helped was that she remain strictly anonymous in the process. Shoot, even *I* didn't know half of the things she'd done for our town over the years.

"Maybe she will," Grace said. "I just don't get it, Suzanne. What kind of pressure could a pie shop owner be under that would make her take her own life?"

"You're kidding, right? Opening up a new business, especially one that deals with food, is a major headache from start to finish. I don't know about her state of finances, but even with my divorce settlement from Max, there were some really lean times at the donut shop, as if I have to remind you."

"No, I remember it all too well," Grace said.

"Not only that, but who knows what really goes on in someone else's mind. I've been shocked by the number of folks plagued by depression over the years, including celebrities who didn't seem to have a care in the world. Sometimes I'm actually glad that I'm not rich and famous. Who needs the scrutiny from the world?"

"I wouldn't mind the rich part, but I agree with you that fame must be highly overrated. How's Gabby taking all of this?"

"You know Gabby. She's hard to read, but she's housing Leanne until this mess is straightened out."

"Isn't that what you do for family?"

"It's certainly what most folks do," I acknowledged, "but Gabby is the one who made such a point about Leanne not being a blood relative. I think when she sensed that I was about to offer to take her in myself, Gabby knew that she had to step up, and to her credit, that's exactly what she did. Anyway, I'm not here to talk about Maggie Moore. Why is Stephen Grant asking me about you? Have you two finally severed your ties to each other?"

"That's an odd way of putting a breakup, Suzanne," Grace said.

"Okay then, we'll use your choice of words. Have you two finally ended things between you?"

"Well, Stephen has," she said with a shrug.

"I'm so sorry," I said, reaching out to pat my friend's shoulder. She'd had more than her share of losers in her love life in the past, but I thought her relationship with Stephen might actually stick.

"Don't be. I've decided not to accept his decision," she said lightheartedly.

"What? Grace, you can't do that. If he doesn't want to be with you, you can't just *make* him."

"That's where you're wrong," she said as she stood and started pacing. "If I refuse to acknowledge the breakup, then it hasn't really happened yet, at least as far as I'm concerned."

"You're not serious, are you?" I looked into my best friend's gaze, but I couldn't honestly tell if she was pulling my leg or not.

"I'm dead serious," Grace said. "He told me we should take a break from each other to get a little perspective, I respectfully disagreed, and that's where we left things."

"I can't imagine this is going to work," I said. "You know that I love you like a sister, but I think you're off track on this one."

"Stephen thinks the same thing, but I'll show you both." Grace said it with absolutely no animosity toward me, or her ex, or not-so-ex, boyfriend, either.

It was clear that she'd made up her mind. "If that's your stand, then I've got your back. What's our game plan to win him back?" I asked. If Grace was going to be crazy, then I was going to be right there with her. After all, it was easy to stick with people when they were winning, rational, and sweet. It was when the entire world was against them that it really counted, at least in my book. That was when the true definition of friendship took over. Grace might get knocked down, but I was going to be right there beside her, fighting until the end and helping her get right back up off the ground.

"Are you really on board with me?" she asked me with a twinkle in her eyes.

"You bet I am. The poor man won't even know what hit him. So, what did you have in mind?"

"I haven't really gotten that far yet," she said. "I'm open to suggestions."

"You could invite him to have a nice dinner here with you tonight," I said. "I'll even cook for you." Grace was many things, but a good cook was not among the skills listed on her résumé.

"I appreciate the offer, but how am I supposed to get him over here on such short notice?" she asked me.

"You could always tell him that you've given his suggestion some thought, and you'd like the opportunity to discuss it further with him," I said.

"I have no intention of doing that though, right?" she asked. "Isn't that kind of ambushing him?"

"I suppose, but do you really want him back?"

"Of course I do. Okay then, an ambush it is. Suzanne, do you really think we can pull this off by tonight?"

"I don't think we have much choice. After all, you don't want to let too much time go by before you act, and I happen to be free tonight. What do you say?"

"You're on," she said. "Let me call him and set something up." Grace took out her cell phone, but she didn't make any move to use it immediately. "Suzanne, I'm as nervous as a schoolgirl."

"I understand completely," I said. "Would you like me to step outside so you can have some privacy?"

"Do you mind?"

"Not at all. I'll be right out there if you need me." I gave her a quick hug, and then I left her to her own devices. I didn't envy Grace making that particular call, and once again, I knew just how lucky I was to have Jake in my life. I knew he was working at the moment, but I thought I'd give him a call and leave him a voicemail anyway. Maybe it would make him smile when he heard it.

I nearly dropped my phone when he picked up on the first ring. "Suzanne, how do you do that?"

"Do what?" I asked. "I didn't think you were supposed to be using your phone."

"Our boss is in a meeting, so we've got ten minutes free. I was just about to call you myself. How's life in April Springs?"

I thought about telling him about Maggie's suicide, but why put a damper on one of the few opportunities I had to speak with my husband while he was away? "Pretty much business as usual," I said. "How's it going with you?"

"Well, I hate to admit it, but I was wrong," Jake said.

"So does that mean that I was right? Excellent. I love when that happens."

My husband's laughter was a welcome sound to me. "I'm not talking about you. Evidently our boss has every reason to be paranoid after all. This guy is ramping up his threats, and we're becoming a little concerned that he might be the real deal after all."

"Jake, are you safe?"

He could clearly hear the concern in my voice. "Suzanne, I'm fine. I'm with some of the best people in the South working on this. I couldn't be any safer if I were home with you."

"We'll have to agree to disagree on that," I said. "Just don't take any chances if you can help it."

"Scout's oath," he said. "Listen, I've got to go. Evidently the meeting didn't go so well, so we're heading out. I love you."

"I love you, too," I said, but it was to dead air. He was already gone. I didn't like keeping things from Jake, but it wasn't as though it was a murder. Even then, I might have kept that to myself. After all, there was no use worrying him about something he couldn't do anything about.

I was still staring at my phone when Grace walked out. She had gotten dressed in the interim, donning slacks, a cute top, and some darling shoes. My friend was always a stylish dresser, something that could never be said about me. "Is this a bad time?" she asked me.

"No, it's fine," I said as I slipped my phone back into my pocket. "What did Stephen say?"

"It took a little cajoling, but it worked," she said with a grin. "He's coming by at six." Grace looked at her watch, and then she asked, "Does that give us enough time to get ready?"

"We'll be fine. What's his favorite meal?" I asked.

"He's got pretty pedestrian tastes," Grace allowed. "I'm sure he'd be happy with eggs and toast."

"We can do better than that," I said, thinking about the things I enjoyed making. Lately I'd been into stir-fries, using peppers, onions, chicken, and rice to make the most delightful meals. It was especially easy when I used cooked chicken from the freezer, thawed out first, of course. "How about a nice stir-fry?"

"Could you make a pot pie instead?" she asked me. "I know it's a lot of trouble, but that's his favorite meal of all. He likes it even more than he likes eating at Napoli's."

That was saying something. For me, there was nothing I enjoyed more than eating at my favorite Italian restaurant in Union Square, and not all of it was because of the women who ran the place, the DeAngelis mother and daughters.

"One chicken pot pie coming up," I said. "We don't even have to go to the store. I've got all of the ingredients at home."

"Then let's get started," Grace said.

"Were you wanting to help me in the kitchen?" I asked as calmly as I could.

She laughed at the suggestion. "No, that's your department. I would love to keep you company while you make it, though."

"You've got yourself a deal," I said. "Tell you what. I'll even tell you how I make it so you can at least sound knowledgeable if Stephen asks how it was made."

"Should I lie and tell him that I made it?" Grace asked. She really was desperate to get his approval if she was willing to do that.

"No, but I'm willing to bet that he'll be impressed that you know how it is made. What could it hurt?"

"Exactly. That sounds like a plan to me."

"Why are we adding flour?" Grace asked as she looked over my shoulder. So, it was "we" now.

"It's part of making a white sauce," I explained. I'd melted four tablespoons of butter in the bottom of the pan at low temperature, and now I was sprinkling four tablespoons of flour, salt, and pepper into the mix, making a roux. As I stirred the mixture together over low heat, I said, "This is the sauce that makes everything taste so good. Okay, after the flour, salt, and pepper are mixed into the butter and cooked a little, we take some of the milk we've set aside and add it to the mix once the pan is off the heat, stirring as we go. Would you like to do that yourself?"

"Sure, why not? At least this way I can say with all honesty that I helped." Grace picked up the two-cup measure, a little over half full of 1% milk, and added a small splash to the mix.

"A smidge more," I said as I stirred it in.

Her "smidge" was half the milk, and as I stirred furiously to try my best to eliminate clumping, Grace asked, "Was that too much?"

"It's fine," I said. Once I was happy with everything, I said, "Now add the rest."

She did as I asked, and I immediately cranked up the heat to HIGH.

"Aren't you worried you're going to burn it?" she asked me.

"That's why I'm stirring so quickly," I said as I stared into the bottom of the pan.

"What are you looking for?" Grace asked me as she joined me in my search.

"The first bubble," I said.

In thirty seconds, I saw it and pulled the completed white sauce off of the heat entirely. "Now grab the veggies and add them directly to the sauce." We were using a bag of baby corn, carrots, and asparagus tips cooked in the microwave oven, and as that incorporated, I instructed her to add the chicken, which she'd defrosted and cut into bite-sized chunks herself. Once it was mixed in as well, I covered the pan and set it aside on the counter.

"Now, are you sure you don't want me to make the crust from scratch?" I asked. "It's really no trouble."

"No, let's just use the pie crust you already had."

I didn't normally keep pie dough hanging around, but I'd been working up some new and simple donut recipes, and I liked trying different things, including store-bought crust, or whatever else struck my fancy.

"Spoon the filling into this casserole dish," I told her, and after it was all in place, I placed the crust over the top. "After we trim the edges, we cut a couple of slits to let the steam vent, and it's ready to go into the oven."

"That was so easy," Grace said as she slipped the dish, safely sitting on a pie sheet to catch anything that might bubble over, into the preheated oven.

"It helps if you've done it a couple of hundred times," I answered with a grin, "but you can make it yourself without any help from me the next time."

"I'm not willing to go that far," Grace said. "Now what do we do?"

"Well, I'd say we could make a pie to go with it, but that was my last crust," I said. "How about some banana pudding?"

"That sounds great," she said. "Wow, look at me. I'm cooking."

"Yes you are," I said when her cell phone rang.

"It's Stephen," Grace said as she stepped into the living room.

I didn't mean to eavesdrop, but the cottage wasn't that big, and besides, she was right there. "What? Stephen, that's not fair. I even made dinner. Okay. Sure. Another time." She came back to me frowning. "I suppose you heard all of that?"

"I did. What possible reason does he have for skipping out on dinner?"

"He said that he just got the coroner's report on Maggie Moore," Grace said. "Apparently it wasn't suicide after all.

"Stephen is pretty sure that she was murdered."

CHAPTER 4

"**M**urder? Is he sure?" I asked as I sat down heavily on the living room couch.

"He sounded pretty sure to me."

"How did he even get an autopsy done so quickly?" I asked her. "This just happened a handful of hours ago."

"Evidently the coroner's office is dead at the moment, pardon the expression. They have some kind of new hotshot who prides himself on getting folks on and off his table as quickly as possible."

"Maybe he made a mistake in his rush to judgment," I said. I'd seen the scene myself, and it had surely looked like suicide to me at the time. Then again, it may have been staged to look that way.

"How exactly was she murdered?" I asked. I hadn't seen any signs of blood at the scene, or blunt force trauma, either.

"Some kind of poison, he said."

"Poison? Did he happen to mention what kind killed her?" I asked.

"No. All I know is that Stephen is bailing out on me tonight."

"I understand that, but you have to cut him a little slack this time," I said. "After all, murder takes precedence over everything else in a cop's world."

"I know you're right, but that doesn't mean that I have to like it. Who knows how long he'll be tied up with this case now."

Grace glanced over at me and must have read something in my expression. "Suzanne, why do you have that look on your face?"

"What look?" I asked her as innocently as I could manage.

"You want to dig into this case yourself, don't you?" she asked. "You know what? Count me in, too. If nothing else, if we solve the case quickly enough, Stephen won't be able to duck out on another dinner with me."

"As helpful to the current state of your love life as that might be, that's *not* why I want to investigate," I told her. "Grace, I was right there when the body was discovered, remember? I saw Maggie slumped over with her head down on her desk, and I'm afraid if we don't do something, Leanne is going to hang for the murder, whether she did it or not."

"Why do you say that?"

"Think about it. She was most likely the last person who saw Maggie alive, she was there alone with her when it happened, and with her aunt gone, I've got a suspicion that Leanne gets the pie shop. Don't most small business owners have that kind of arrangement, especially when they're related as well?"

"I wouldn't know," Grace said. "But given the way you put it, she sounds kind of guilty to me."

"True, but you weren't there. I saw her face when she told us her aunt was dead, and I helped steady her. That girl was about to collapse! I just can't believe that young woman is a cold-blooded killer. The woman had me try one of her tarts while her aunt was in the building, and chances are good that Maggie was already dead! Who could be so good at hiding something like that?"

"A psychopath, maybe?" Grace asked.

"Unless I'm way off course, I can't imagine Leanne being one," I said. "The situation at least deserves closer examination."

"Like I said before, I'm in," Grace said as she grabbed her jacket.

"There's only one thing wrong with getting straight to work on the case," I said.

"What's that?"

"We have a chicken pot pie in the oven," I replied.

"Can't we just take it out and start investigating?" she asked me.

"After all that work? It will just take half an hour to finish up, and then we can be on our way," I answered. I was as eager to get on the case as she was, but I was, in many ways, my mother's daughter, and I couldn't let good food go to waste like that. "In the meantime, you can use my computer and see what you can dig up on Maggie Moore and Leanne Halder."

"Suzanne, you really need to upgrade your computer," Grace said twenty minutes later as she rejoined me from the guest bedroom/office upstairs.

"Why? It works well enough for my needs."

"I don't see how," she said in obvious disgust. "At least I know what I'm getting you for Christmas this year."

"It better not be a computer," I said. "Seriously. What I've got works fine. Were you able to find anything out, or was it too antiquated to even use?"

Grace shrugged. "I managed to coax a few things out of it, despite its obvious limitations."

"Are you going to tell me what you uncovered, or are you going to spend the next nine minutes the pot pie needs to stay in the oven to tease me?"

Grace pulled out a notebook as she explained, "I couldn't get your printer to work, so I had to take notes by hand."

"Did you jiggle the cord and hold the power button on for twelve seconds, release it for two, then push it again for six seconds?"

"No, I didn't realize it had a set of crazy start-up instructions," Grace said as she shook her head. "Okay, let's start with Maggie Moore. She was born Margaret Haller and married Clifford Moore twenty years ago."

"When did they get divorced? He's still not married to the woman, is he?" I couldn't imagine anybody putting up with that dour woman for very long, no matter how much he might have loved her initially.

"They're not still married, but they didn't get a divorce," Grace said, raising an eyebrow.

"He died? No wonder she's so sour. I'm starting to feel bad about the way I reacted to her. I can't imagine losing a spouse, can you?"

"No, particularly not in those circumstances."

That sounded a bit cryptic. "How exactly did he die, Grace?"

"Apparently the coroner ended up ruling it an accidental death, but there were a great deal of rumors flying around at the time. It turns out that he was poisoned. Whether it was accidentally or on purpose, no one really knows."

"Poisoned? You're kidding. What are the odds that they would *both* be poisoned?"

"I'd have a really hard time believing that it's just a coincidence," Grace said. "Maggie's sister-in-law has been very vocal for years about her involvement in her brother's death. She's been pestering the district attorney to do something for a very long time, but with no results, at least as far as I can tell."

"So, you think it's possible that Clifford's sister took matters into her own hands and extracted revenge on her own terms, a kind of cold justice?" It sounded outlandish to me, but then again, I knew that folks committed some rather troublesome acts if they felt as though they were avenging a lost loved one.

"I don't know, but we need to talk to her. Her name is

Beatrice Branch, and she lives in Union Square, at least the last time I could find an address for her, that is."

"What else did you uncover?" I asked as I moved into the kitchen and flipped on the oven light. The pie was looking rather grand, and I had a feeling that it wasn't going to need the entire time to bake. That happened sometimes, which was one of the reasons I always hesitated in giving out precise cooking times when I shared my recipes. So many factors could come into play besides the individual quirks that ovens had, like temperature, humidity, and as far as I knew, phases of the moon.

"Maggie has evidently made her share of enemies lately, including her niece."

"Leanne? Is she upset about the way they set up the pie business?"

"I don't know, but Maggie just self-published a recipe book on pie making, and there's a pretty scathing review from someone calling themselves A REAL PIEMAKER calling her a fraud. You have to wonder, given what you discovered, if Leanne left that review after finding out what her aunt had done."

I hated thieves of just about any ilk, but stealing someone else's creative work was massively egregious in my book. I couldn't imagine how I'd feel if someone found *my* donut recipe book, formatted it, and put it up for sale claiming it was their own. All I knew was that it would get ugly the second I found out; there was no doubt about that.

"How's the book selling?" I asked, curious if maybe I should do a recipe book of donuts myself.

"Not very well, judging by its ranking," she said. "It's up in the millions, so I doubt it's sold more than a copy or two."

So maybe that wasn't a great idea after all. I was sure there was more to making a book than I realized, and I wasn't sure I wanted to put in all of that work if no one was even going to buy it. Besides, what if they did? Could someone else put me out of business selling my own donuts to the folks of April Springs? It was something to think about, anyway.

"Were you able to find out anything else?"

"Nothing specific. For a woman in her early twenties, Leanne Haller has a remarkably low profile online. It doesn't matter, though. I'm starting to come around to your way of thinking. The Internet can't take the place of actually talking to real people," Grace said.

"That surprises me to hear you say that," I said. "I thought you were the New Age of Information guru?"

"It's got its place, I'm not denying it, but what we do face to face can be a lot more valuable. You can't read an expression online or judge someone by the way they act, their tone of voice, the particular manner in which they move."

"I'm glad you agree with me," I said. I checked on the pie again. It was definitely finished. Grabbing some hot-pads, I reached in and pulled the pot pie out, placing it on the cooling rack after removing the cookie sheet. I was glad I'd added that at the end, since there had been some definite bubbling over during the cooking process, and it would be easier to clean that than the bottom of my oven.

"That smells and looks amazing," Grace said as she leaned a little closer for another whiff. "I can't believe we actually made it."

"We can come back and have it for dinner later, if you'd like," I suggested.

"Why can't we eat it now?" she asked with a grin.

"One, it's way too hot, and two, I like to let it cool for at least thirty minutes so all of the flavors can come together."

"That's all well and good, but what do we do for thirty minutes? It barely gives us time to drive to Union Square, let alone interview anyone and get back before it's stone cold."

I had to laugh. "You're awfully invested in eating this pot pie, aren't you?"

"Hey, I helped make it, so of course I want to take part in appreciating the final result. It's just a shame Stephen won't be able to enjoy it."

"You could always take him a piece later after we've eaten," I suggested.

"Do you think that might be pushing it?" she asked me hesitantly.

"Grace, you're rejecting the man's demand that you two break up. Do you honestly believe that feeding him is the thing that's going to push him too far?"

"No, I suppose you're right. Okay, we have thirty minutes. What should we do with the time?"

"Let's go see if we can't have a little chat with Leanne. I'd like to ask her more about her aunt, and that pie-making cookbook, too. If she's the one who left that review, it might mean that she had another reason to kill her aunt that we're just learning about."

"Gabby, we need to speak with Leanne," I said as she answered the door at her place. It had taken something pretty major to get me to go there, and Grace had been even more reluctant to go. As turbulent as my relationship with Gabby was at times, it was full of warm and fuzzy feelings compared to how she and my best friend got along.

"You can't," Gabby said, her brow furrowed as deeply as I'd ever seen it in my life.

"Come on," I said. "This isn't the time to dig your heels in. Unless we miss our guess, she might be railroaded for murder." It suddenly occurred to me that Gabby wasn't aware of the chief of police's new information. I had just broken the news rather heartlessly if that was the case. "I'm sorry. You didn't know what they uncovered about Maggie's death, did you?"

Gabby shook her head, frowning. "Of course I knew. Did

you honestly think that you were the only person in this town with connections in law enforcement?"

"How did Leanne take it? I'd love to talk to her."

"So would I," Gabby said. "When I told you that you *couldn't* talk to her, I meant it *literally*. She's with Chief Grant even as we speak."

"I'm surprised you didn't tag along," Grace said. Maybe it wasn't the most tactful way of saying it, and there was a chance that Grace brought some of Gabby's animosity upon herself, but I wasn't about to point that out to either one of them.

"Don't you think I tried? He threatened to arrest me for obstruction of justice if I didn't back down! Can you imagine? I've known that young man since he was just a pup, and he had the gall to refuse my simple request to accompany my niece to the station."

I could well imagine that particular conversation, and while Stephen Grant was currently in my doghouse, I had to give him credit for standing up to Gabby. It wasn't something many folks in April Springs would be willing, or able, to do. "He didn't come right out and arrest her, did he?" I asked as gently as I could manage it.

"No, at least not while she was here in my home. The chief said that there were some topics he needed to cover with her and that they should go back to his office. I tried to tell Leanne not to go, but she wouldn't listen to me! She said she was innocent and had nothing to fear from the police. What a naïve young woman! She's going to land in jail despite herself."

I wasn't going to address either the young woman's guilt or her innocence, and I was about to say something very carefully worded about being there for her when Grace asked, "How do you know that she *didn't* do it?"

Gabby whirled around and faced Grace with rage in her eyes.

"Are you accusing my niece of murder? Be very careful about your next words, Grace Gauge."

Grace started to stammer under the attack, so I stepped in. "Gabby, the *only* thing we want to do is to find the truth. That's why Grace and I have decided to dig into Maggie's murder."

"Good. I was hoping you'd say that. Suzanne, I want to help," Gabby said, shocking both Grace and me with her offer. What could she possibly add to our investigation? Gabby Williams certainly wasn't the most empathetic person in our town, and I doubted anyone would open up to her like they did with me.

Still, upon further consideration, there might be a *few* things she could help us with.

"Excellent," I said, noting the disbelief on Grace's face as I accepted Gabby's offer. "You could start by answering some questions we have, but I need to warn you, they might be painful to hear. Just remember why we're doing this."

"For goodness' sake, I'm not some delicate flower," she said. "Why are we standing out here? Come inside."

I started to follow her in when Grace grabbed my arm. "Suzanne, what are you doing?" she asked me softly.

"Just follow my lead," I whispered.

I was about to say more when Gabby turned back toward us. "Ladies, you mustn't dawdle. Time is of the essence."

It was no real surprise that Gabby's place was as neat as a pin and very well furnished. Not for the first time did I realize that she must have had a significant markup on the items she sold. How else could she afford such splendor? It was no wonder most folks in April Springs had never been inside Gabby's house. One look at her furnishings would surely have made them all suspect that they'd been paying inflated prices for far too long.

"Tea?" Gabby asked.

"It's sweet of you to offer, but we really are on a time crunch here," Grace said. Was she talking about the case itself or the chicken pot pie cooling on the rack back at my cottage? Either way, I agreed with her. It was best to get this interview over with as quickly as possible. We needed to ask our questions, get any answers we could, and then get out of there while I still had some kind of relationship with the woman, my next-door business neighbor and sometime friend.

Gabby seemed to be about to protest our refusal, but after a moment, she appeared to accept it, albeit reluctantly. "Very well. What would you like to know?"

"Tell us about Clifford Moore," I said.

Gabby didn't answer right away. She took a few moments to mull over her answer before she spoke, and when she finally did, it was clear that she spoke with a heavy heart. "I knew that would come up again. Maggie didn't poison that man, no matter what that witch of a sister of his might claim."

"I take it you're not Beatrice Branch's biggest fan," I said. I glanced over at Grace, who was sitting back and taking it all in. No doubt she'd learned her lesson earlier, so I was going to take the brunt of the fallout from this interrogation. I can't say that I blamed her, given their past history.

"She's a shrew, and if anyone poisoned Cliff, it was most likely her."

"Why would she kill her own brother?" Grace asked. So, I'd misinterpreted her game plan after all. It appeared that she was quite willing to wade into the fray herself.

"Insurance money," Gabby said, "and a rather substantial family inheritance."

"Wouldn't Maggie inherit all of that as his wife?" I asked.

"No. The truth of the matter is that she didn't get much at all from the estate. In fact, that evidence helped ease the police's minds that she had no financial motive to kill Clifford."

"But did she realize that at the time?" Grace asked.

"Realize what?"

The Donut Mysteries: Prejury Proof

"That she was going to get the short end of the straw," she answered.

"Of course she knew," Gabby said, and then, after frowning for a moment, she added, "At least I believe she knew. It's a little too late to ask her about it now, isn't it?"

"But there's no real financial gain for Beatrice with Maggie's death, is there?" I asked.

"I'm not so sure about that," Gabby answered. "From what I understand, the estate was rather complicated, and there were provisions made that, after a certain period of time, Maggie could file a petition to the trust to increase her portion of her inheritance."

"When was that cutoff date?" I asked.

"Sometime next week, I believe," Gabby said.

"We'll look into that," I answered. "Do you know anyone else who might want to hurt Maggie? Think about it. It could be important."

"Well, besides Ashton Belle, I can't think of a soul." She was biting her lip as she said it, and I wondered if we were getting the entire truth out of her. Why would Gabby hide someone else from us if they might be a viable suspect in her cousin's murder?

"Who is Ashton Belle," I asked, "and why does that name sound so familiar?"

"He's a banker in Maple Hollow. I'm not sure why there was so much animosity between them, but they really couldn't stand one another. You'd have to ask him."

"Believe me, we will," I said. "Is there anyone else?" I wanted to give Gabby one last chance to come clean with us before I dug it out another way.

"Not that I know of, but you should ask Leanne. She knew Maggie better than the rest of us."

It was a perfect opening to ask another question I'd been

41

dying to pose. "Gabby, what did Leanne think about Maggie's pie-maker's recipe cookbook?"

"You knew about that?" Gabby asked, sharing an incredulous look with both of us.

"The more important question is what did Leanne think about it?" Grace asked her.

"As far as I know, Leanne doesn't know a thing about it, and I plan for it to stay that way."

"Gabby, what makes you think she didn't know? There's a scathing review of it online, and it sounded as though Leanne might have written it herself, especially if she were unhappy about it being published in the first place."

Gabby looked at me smugly before she replied. "It *was* very well written, don't you think?"

"You wrote that review yourself, didn't you?" I asked her.

"Yes," she answered defiantly. "Maggie needed to unpublish it and give the credit to Leanne," Gabby said. "When she wouldn't listen to reason, I decided to make sure that *no one* bought it. Look at the sales rank. She's probably only sold a copy or two since it's been for sale."

I thought that might have something more to do with how difficult it was for new writers of any kind to break in, based on what I'd read online, but if she wanted to think that she was a giant killer, far be it from me to set her straight.

I was still thinking about my next question when Grace surprised me by asking, "Gabby, you said that Chief Grant came by to speak with Leanne. What I'm curious about is why the chief of police didn't want to interview you, too." I found it odd to hear her refer to Stephen Grant as the chief of police, but then again, I knew how tense things were between them at the moment.

"Because he knows I would never kill my own cousin," Gabby said. She looked equal parts angry and hurt that Grace had even asked the question. Gabby was clearly about to protest further when her cell phone rang. After quickly glancing at her caller ID, she said, "I have to take this. Will you two excuse me?"

"We need to be on our way, anyway," I said. "Thanks for your help."

Gabby held one finger in the air as she answered her call. "Don't be in such a rush." After a moment, she said, "Give me one second," to whoever was calling her before she turned back to us. "Use me, ladies. I can be a great asset in your investigation."

"We will do our best," I said as we finally made our escape.

Once we were outside, Grace said, "I've really got to hand it to you, Suzanne. I thought you'd lost your mind when you asked her to help us investigate, but it turned out to be a stroke of sheer brilliance. How much of what she told us do you believe?"

"Enough to dig into everything she brought up. I have a feeling she was holding a name back from us, don't you?"

"She did kind of hesitate when you asked her," Grace said. "What do we do now?"

"Well, it's time to cut that pot pie if you're still interested."

"Just try to stop me," Grace said, and we both got into my Jeep and headed back to the cottage.

For now, the investigation was going to have to wait.

My stomach was grumbling for some good old-fashioned home cooking, and it was about to get it.

CHAPTER 5

"Wow, I'm quite the chef, aren't I?" Grace asked after she took her first bite of our pot pie. "Who knew I had it in me?"

"I suspected as much all along," I said with a smile. The truth was that the meal was delightful, and I didn't think the store-bought pie crust took away from the dish at all. Sometimes it was nice taking a shortcut or two, not that making pie crust was all that arduous. Combine a little flour, salt, butter, and ice water, and in a few easy steps, you had crust, but there were times I didn't want to go through the process, especially waiting for the mixture to chill enough so it could be rolled out. Besides, I made things from scratch all of the time at my donut shop, so a shortcut every now and then at home was perfectly fine with me.

"All I needed was the right teacher," Grace said, returning my grin with one of her own.

As we ate, I asked, "Would it be okay with you if we talked about Maggie's murder while we dine on this fine cuisine?"

"I'm perfectly fine with it," she said. "From the way you've described her, I can't believe we don't have more suspects than we do."

"We just started digging, though. Who knows how many more will turn up in the course of our investigation?"

"That's a happy thought, isn't it?" she said sarcastically.

"The woman had a way of making a truly horrid first impression, and if we've learned anything about her so far, she never did anything to change people's expectations of her afterwards. Still, she didn't deserve to die that way. I can't imagine someone wanting to kill me enough to poison me."

"You saw the body," Grace said after taking another bite. "Did it appear to you that she'd been poisoned?"

"I don't know. What does a person who's been poisoned look like?" I asked her.

"I guess I expected you to be able to tell," Grace said with a shrug.

"No, it appeared to me that she'd just slumped over after having a heart attack or something like that," I answered after giving it a few moments' thought.

"And what does that look like?"

"I have no idea," I admitted. "I haven't seen all that many natural deaths in my life."

"But plenty of homicides," Grace replied.

"Way too many," I agreed. "So far, as much as I'd like to, we can't rule out Leanne, no matter what impression I may have given Gabby that we were fighting for her niece's exoneration."

"You handled that rather deftly, I must admit."

"If you'll recall, I told her that we wanted the truth, not necessarily to save Leanne."

"I know, but the subtext was awfully subtle," Grace pointed out.

"True, but what good would it have done us if I'd told her that Leanne has to be one of our prime suspects? Her subjugation at the pie shop was bad enough, but if Maggie really did steal Leanne's recipes and then sold them online as her own work, it crossed so many lines, I don't even know where to begin. If Leanne knew about what she'd done, I have a hunch it would have made her pretty angry, even if she were perfectly fine with working for Maggie and not being a co-owner of Sky High Pie. So we know that Leanne had motive and loads of opportunity.

As a matter of fact, her proximity to Maggie, and in theory her bottle of pills as well, is the single worst piece of evidence against her at the moment, at least as far as I'm concerned."

"Until we know what kind of poison was used to kill her," Grace said, "we won't be able to determine if she had access to it or not, so the means of the crime are still up in the air."

"I guess the next thing we need to do is find out what exactly it was that she died of," I said.

"Well, I'm seeing Stephen soon," Grace replied. "Maybe *he'll* tell me."

"Grace, remember, you aren't delivering him food in order to interrogate him. You're trying to convince him to stay with you."

"Why can't I do both?" she asked impishly.

"No offense, but I'm not even sure that *you're* that good, and that's saying something."

"We'll see. I won't bring it up, but if he does, I'll push him on it a little. Don't worry, it will be fine."

"I just don't want you to do anything to ruin your chances of working things out with Stephen, even if it means advancing our investigation."

"I won't," Grace said firmly, and I knew from her tone of voice that I needed to drop the subject.

"Okay, let's talk about who else might have done it if Leanne turns out to be innocent. First of all, Beatrice Branch *has* to be on the list."

"She probably had more reason to kill Maggie than Leanne did," Grace said. "Money and revenge make a pretty powerful pair of motives."

"Yes, but we can't forget about the mysterious Ashton Belle of Maple Hollow. Clearly there was some real animosity between them."

"But was it enough to move him to murder?" Grace asked after taking her last bite.

"There's only one way to find that out," I said. "Tomorrow we'll have to ask him."

"Why not tonight?" Grace asked me. "We're finished eating, and the night is still young." Then she glanced at the clock. "Except for you, anyway. Your hours can be a real inconvenience to our investigations at times, can't they?"

"Sorry for the inconvenience," I said with a grin. When we'd been teenagers working as cashiers at the grocery store after school, whenever we'd have a customer rant at us about anything that was not in any way our fault, we'd say our catchphrase, "sorry for the inconvenience," which in fact meant something else entirely, more along the lines of saying "go bark at the moon." Delivered with a bright, albeit fake, smile, it usually mollified the customer while still allowing us to retain a bit of self-respect as well.

"Right back at you," she said happily. "So, at the moment, we have three suspects."

"Four, if you count Gabby," I said.

"Are we *counting* Gabby?" Grace asked me.

"Grace, you weren't there. I have to tell you, there was some real friction between them, and Maggie seemed to be able to push Gabby's buttons pretty easily. I don't like to admit it, but she *could* have lashed out at her."

"Maybe with a tire iron, but with poison?" Grace asked. "That doesn't seem like her style to me. Does it to you?"

"No, you're right, not ordinarily, but we still can't take Gabby's name off our list of suspects entirely, even if we believe that she would never use poison. It's much too subtle for her taste."

"What about Paige Hill?" Grace asked me.

"What about her? Oh, are you talking about the little squabble she had with Maggie out in front of her shop?"

"Surely that's not grounds for murder, though, is it?"

"No, probably not," I said. "It *was* pretty heated when I got there, though."

Grace frowned for a moment before she spoke. "Do you honestly think Paige could have killed her, especially with poison?"

"No," I answered fairly quickly. "That's the thing. Whoever did it must have known Maggie for a while, and fairly well."

"Why do you say that?"

"Think about it. Who knew she was even taking medication for her heart? Besides, poison comes from a slow hate, not a quick burst of anger. To top that off, who was close enough to poison her without causing suspicion on her part? No matter how she ingested whatever it was that killed her, Maggie wouldn't exactly accept something from a stranger, would she? It would have to be someone she knew fairly well."

"So we still have just three main suspects, if we put Gabby and Paige in the second tier. To be fair, that's better than the way we start with most of our investigations," Grace said as she stood and grabbed our empty plates.

"Don't worry about those. I'll do them later," I said.

"You weren't under the impression that I was going to actually *wash* them, were you?" she asked with a hint of laughter in her voice. "I was just going to rinse them off and leave them in the sink for you to deal with yourself."

"That's the girl I know and love," I said happily. Even in situations dire and without much hope, I loved being with Grace. There was just something about her that made the good times better and the bad ones not nearly as bleak as they might have been. I supposed that was what friendship really was, when all was said and done. "Let me put some pot pie in some Tupperware for you. How much would you like to take him? There's quite a bit left here."

"How about half?"

"What should we do with the rest of it?" I asked her as I did as she instructed.

"I thought I'd take it home with me and have it again tomorrow night, if you don't mind," she said sheepishly. "Besides, Stephen could never eat all of that in one sitting."

"That sounds like a plan to me," I said. After I had the portions divided up equally, I handed them both to Grace.

"Any chance you'd like to go with me when I deliver this?" she asked me a little sheepishly as she headed for the door.

"Do you really want an audience?" I asked her.

"No, I suppose not."

I stopped her from leaving. "Grace, what's wrong?"

"Nothing. I'm fine."

"Are you honestly that nervous about talking to Stephen?" I asked her. Could it be possible that my friend, normally so full of self-assurance and bravado, was actually anxious about talking to her boyfriend?

"Kind of," she said in a meek voice I hadn't heard in ages. "Suzanne, am I being ridiculous? Do I really *want* someone in my life who doesn't want to be with me?"

"If you honestly believe that, then no, you don't. But what if he's just feeling the pressure of his job and taking it out on you? If you two belong together and you just roll over and take this breakup at face value, will you ever be able to get a relationship with him back again? I guess the real question is what you think his underlying motivation is for suggesting you two split up."

"That's it, right on the money." She looked at me steadily for a moment before asking, "When did you suddenly get so wise?"

I had to laugh. "Grace, it's easy to see things in *other* people's relationships. It's when we come to our own lives that we're usually blind to the truth."

"That's certainly true enough for me," she said. To my surprise, Grace put the two containers down on the table by the front door and hugged me fiercely before she left. "Suzanne, it's good to have you in my life."

"Right back at you," I said. "After you speak with Stephen, I want you to come straight back here, no matter how late it might be. Do you understand?"

"What if you're already asleep? I may have to wait awhile if he's still talking to Leanne. We both know how long those sessions can last."

"I don't care what time it is, wake me up if you have to," I said. "I'll be on the couch, either watching television or snoring my head off, but either way, I want to know how it goes."

"Yes, ma'am," she said with a mock salute before she collected the containers of food again and left the cottage.

After Grace was gone, I thought about the vulnerability I'd just seen in my friend. She was usually so strong, so steadfast, that I didn't always realize that deep down, she was just like the rest of us, fragile and delicate on levels that most folks never saw. I hoped things worked out for her. She deserved to have someone in her life to cherish and someone to cherish her in return.

I was dozing off in front of a television show I didn't care about, mostly turned on for the company of the sound of other voices in my empty cottage, when someone rang my doorbell. I knew instantly that it wasn't Grace. I'd left the door unlocked on purpose, and she would have tried that before hitting the doorbell, since she knew that I was expecting her.

"Paige, what are you doing here?" I asked the bookstore owner as I opened the door to find her standing there.

"I'm sorry. It's late for you, isn't it?" Paige asked, suddenly very apologetic. In her late twenties, she looked much younger, almost elfin in appearance, but something was clearly troubling her.

"Nonsense. Come on in," I said as I stepped aside to let her in. She took a sniff of the air. "That smells wonderful."

"I'd offer you some, but I'm afraid it's all gone."

"I wasn't hinting around for a free meal," she said with a weary smile. "Suzanne, I think I might be in trouble."

"What's going on?" I asked. The bookshop owner certainly had my attention. She hadn't been in town very long, at least not compared to many of the locals, but we'd become friends, and I hated seeing her so upset.

"You know about most of it. That fight I had with Maggie Moore out in front of all of April Springs is coming back to haunt me already."

After we sat in the living room, I asked, "Would you like some coffee or sweet tea?" I had the tea in the fridge, but I could make the coffee in two shakes if she wanted some. There were times when a beverage helped lubricate conversation, and it didn't necessarily have to be alcohol. Just holding something in your hands, having something to stare at, was often enough of an icebreaker for most folks.

"No, thanks. I'm good."

"Why do you think you're in trouble? I had a fight with Maggie too, but I haven't seen any repercussions from it."

"That's because you haven't been open since everybody found out she was poisoned. I swear, my shop was so empty I had to close early just to keep folks from noticing. Is that the way things work in April Springs?"

"I've gone through more than my share of lulls myself," I said, remembering the sting from the most recent one when I'd worried about losing my shop altogether. In fact, I was still dancing a thin edge, not quite breaking even yet but not going too much farther into the hole. "It will pass."

"I hope so. Suzanne, I didn't kill that woman. I barely even knew her."

"I'm in the same boat you are. Just out of curiosity, why were you two squabbling this morning?"

"You didn't hear any of that?" she asked.

"No, that's why I'm asking. Listen, if you'd rather not say, I'm fine with that."

"As a matter of fact," she said a bit guiltily, "we were fighting about you."

"About me?" I asked, stunned by the revelation. "Why were you fighting about me?"

"I didn't like the way she treated you, and I told her so. I won't stand idly by and let my friends be attacked by *anybody*, but I'm afraid I just made things worse."

I smiled at her and patted her hand. "I appreciate you defending me."

"For all the good it did either one of us," she said a little morosely.

"As far as I'm concerned, it really is the thought that counts," I told her. "You shouldn't lose any sleep over this. It's going to be all right."

"Do you really think so?" she asked, the hope aching in her voice.

"I *choose* to believe it," I said with a gentle smile. "Besides, there's really nothing we can do about it either way, is there?"

"I suppose not," Paige said as she stood. "Well, I won't keep you any longer. I just wanted to see a friendly face."

"I'm glad you came by, and remember, this face is always there for you," I said, "and the rest of me, too."

"Thanks. Right back at you."

"I'm curious about something. Overall, business seems

strong," I said. "How are you managing to do it in this Internet age when everybody seems to buy their books online?"

"Not everybody, thankfully," she said. "I like to think most folks appreciate a knowledgeable bookseller who has actually read a lot of the books they want to know about, or at the very least, some of the author's works. I can usually give pretty solid advice on what someone might like and something they might steer away from."

"That's fascinating. How on earth can you do that?"

"Well, take you, for example. I know a great deal about you simply based on the books you've bought from me in the past. I know for a fact that you love cozy mysteries, but you wouldn't touch a slasher novel on a bet. You like contemporary romance, but you don't care for Regency. You enjoy a good biography, no matter what the time period, but you wouldn't touch a war novel with a ten-foot pole if I were giving them away. Based on all of that, I can usually come up with a fairly safe reading list you might like. I'm not saying that you don't enjoy a Stephen King novel now and then, but it's not your bread-and-butter reading material. How close am I?"

"Probably a little too close for comfort," I admitted. "That's fascinating. I had no idea you were paying that close attention."

"My entire business plan is based on knowing my customers and my offerings," she said.

"Do someone else," I suggested, fascinated by the process.

"I'm sorry, but I can't do that, not even for you. I respect the privacy of my customers too much. I'm not sure I would even divulge anyone else's reading list with a court order. There are some things worth going to jail for."

"I can respect that. So, that's enough to keep you afloat?"

"Well, I also host as many book clubs as I can, and I'm trying to get more author signings, but it's getting tougher and tougher to book those these days."

"Maybe we should have a Books and Donuts Festival. We could call it Knead and Read," I suggested purely in jest. "Between the two of us, we'd bring folks in from miles around."

"If you're at all serious, I'm in if you are," she said. "It might just provide the boost we both need. What do you say?"

She'd caught me a little off guard with her enthusiasm, but it was true. I could certainly use the customers. "After this murder business is cleared up, let's talk more about it."

"You've got a deal," she said. "I'm glad I came here this evening. I feel loads better."

"I'm glad I could help," I said, and then I caught a sudden movement on my front porch. Who was out there now, and more importantly, what did they want?

CHAPTER 6

"**G**RACE, IS THAT YOU? WHAT are you doing lurking out here on my front porch?" I asked her as Paige and I stepped outside together. I had to admit that I felt a lot braver having the bookstore owner with me, though I suspected she wasn't armed with anything more than a nail file, just like me. Still, there was safety in numbers, or at least it felt that way to me.

"I didn't want to interrupt. I saw you had company," Grace said, clearly deflated about her meeting with Stephen. And why shouldn't she be? She hadn't been gone nearly long enough to have a meaningful conversation with her beau.

"I was just leaving," Paige said. "You've got yourself a terrific best friend there," she told Grace happily.

"Don't I know it," Grace replied with a slight smile.

After Paige was gone, I asked her, "So, what happened?"

"He wouldn't even see me," she said, her words tumbling out in a rush.

"Take a deep breath and tell me all about it," I said. "Are you sure it wasn't 'couldn't see you' instead of 'wouldn't'?"

"It's pretty much the same thing, isn't it?" Grace asked.

"You know how he gets when he's working," I said. "Jake is the same way. It's not that they don't care for us, it's just that there are more pressing things on their minds. To be fair, we get that way sometimes ourselves."

"Are you actually defending him?" Grace asked me, clearly ready for an argument if I was interested in participating.

"Hang on a second. I'm on your side, remember? Now, tell me exactly what happened."

"I never even got to speak with him. He left standing orders that short of the presence of blood, he wasn't to be disturbed. He's still locked up in the interrogation room with Leanne."

"Which we suspected. Take it easy, Grace. Did you at least leave him the pot pie and a nice note?"

"Well, I did half of that," she said with a shrug.

"Which half?"

"I left the pie. Let *him* figure out who it was from." After a moment, she shrugged. "I don't know why I let that man get under my skin like that."

"Maybe it's because you care about him," I suggested.

"Yeah, maybe. Suzanne, are you dead set on going right to sleep?"

I glanced at the clock. While it was true that I could probably have nodded off, it felt as though Grace wanted to chat. "I'm wide awake at the moment. Do you want to talk about what happened this evening?"

My friend chuckled, but there was no joy in it. "That's actually the *last* thing I want to do. I suspect I was a bit of a petulant brat earlier, so we don't need to revisit that."

"Then what did you have in mind?"

"If it's all the same to you, I'd like to have a look at that pie shop," she said.

"So would I, but it's probably got crime scene tape around it now," I answered.

"Maybe, but I'd still love to have a look at the building itself. Am I just being silly?"

"Not at all," I said as I grabbed my keys. "Let's go."

"Thanks for indulging me," she said.

"Hey, what are friends for?"

On the short drive over to the pie shop, or what had been promised to be a pie shop, at any rate, Grace got a call on her cell phone. "It's Stephen," she said. "What should I do?"

"I don't know. Here's a crazy thought. Why don't you answer it?"

She laughed, the tension suddenly broken. "Yeah, that sounds like a plan to me."

"Do you want me to pull over so you can have some privacy?" I offered as we neared Donut Hearts. That was one of the great things about my business; it was literally a stone's throw away from my cottage, which made my daily commute, if you could even call it that, a dream.

"No, you've been there for it all, including the bumps along the way. You might as well hear this, too."

"Then you'd better answer your phone before he gives up," I suggested.

At least she didn't put it on speaker, so I didn't have to hear his responses as well. Somehow it felt a little less like eavesdropping that way.

"Yes, it was from me. Of course I baked it myself. Yes, Suzanne helped, too. You're welcome. How's the case going?" she asked as she winked at me. "Really? Wow, that's hard to believe. Yes. Okay. Tomorrow night. Yes, I'll pencil it in. Thanks for calling. You're welcome," she repeated before hanging up. I couldn't tell in the darkness, but was she actually blushing a little at the end?

"That went well, didn't it? I can't believe you nearly blew it asking about the case," I chided her as I continued to drive the short way to the pie shop site.

"Hey, I sensed an opening, and I took it."

When no more details were forthcoming, I asked her, "So,

are you going to share what you learned, or are you going to keep it to yourself?"

"As suspected, the poison was in the pills. More specifically, it was on them. Have you ever heard of vanalaxis macromium?"

"No, not that I can recall. What is it?"

"Apparently it's a common additive to a great many household cleaning products, and it's pretty toxic stuff when it's distilled down to a concentrated form. Over half of the pills they found on the scene were doused with the stuff in some pretty high concentrations. It turns out that Maggie Moore was playing a rigged game of Russian Roulette every time she took her meds."

"Wow, that's crazy, isn't it?"

"I'll say. Why would anybody do it that way?" Grace asked me.

"What do you mean?" I asked her.

"Well, if *I* were going to poison someone, I would have either coated just one pill or the entire lot of them. That way I'd either make the police think it was some kind of random act of violence, or they'd have to struggle to find what killed her."

"I never realized you had such a devious mind," I said as I shook my head. "That would have never even occurred to me."

"That's why there are two of us," she said with a smile. "Unfortunately, the poison is used in a great many things, though someone had to know how to reduce the liquid to the point where it was fatal."

"That might narrow the list down a little," I said, "but the problem is that with the Internet, you can find out how to do just about anything these days."

"Or in a book," Grace said a little ominously.

"You're not thinking about Paige again, are you?" I asked.

"No, but she could have sold a book about poison to someone in town. We could at least ask her."

"We could, but I know for a fact that she wouldn't tell us. She takes her customers' privacy very seriously."

"Even when it comes to murder?"

"Even then," I replied.

We turned left onto Viewmont Avenue and headed toward the crime scene. Just down the road from the building my father had left me was the pie shop, or at least the place where the pie shop would have been. Who knew if it would ever get off the ground now? I looked over at the police station/jail combination building and saw that it was still a busy place, even given the hour of night. Well, it probably wasn't that late for most folks, but for me, it was getting awfully close to bedtime. I'd try to stretch it a bit since Grace and I were working on a case, but I had to get at least six hours of sleep a night if I could manage it. Any less and I'd be nearly worthless the next day, and with the hot oil and some of the other things I dealt with on a regular basis, it was probably a good idea to be sharp and on my game.

"I hope she goes ahead with it," Grace said as I pulled in back of the building. There was decent parking there, and my Jeep wouldn't advertise our presence, either. After all, there was no sense broadcasting to all of April Springs that we were snooping around, even though I knew that most folks wouldn't be all that surprised to learn that we were digging into the murder. Unfortunately, over the years, Grace and I had developed reputations for doing just that sort of thing.

I grabbed my heavy-duty flashlight and got out. "Let's have a look around, shall we?"

As we walked toward the rear entrance of the building, I thought I saw something, or someone, in the shadows. After shining my light, though, I couldn't see anyone or anything.

"Did you just see something, too?" Grace asked me.

"I thought I might have. Was it a person, or was there any chance that it could it have been a dog or a cat?"

"If it was somebody's pet, it was an awfully big one. If you ask me, it had to be a person," she said. "Come on. Let's go check it out."

Before I could stop her, Grace headed off on the path that led around to the front of the building and, more importantly, Viewmont Avenue, which was much closer to the police station than I really wanted to be.

"Wait for me," I said as I hurried to catch up with her.

As we hurried around the building, I noticed something that I'd missed on my previous visit. Was that another way into the building? It was easy enough to overlook it, especially in the daylight hours, since there was a huge clump of overgrown bushes hiding it from view. Only the reflected beam of my flashlight had given me any idea that it might even be there. For such a compact building, it had quite a few doors. The front door was clearly for the public, while the back one served as an employee and delivery entrance, so what was the side door for, originally? I'd want to take a look at it, but not until we figured out who had been creeping around the building when they shouldn't have been there. I knew there was a bit of irony there, since we weren't exactly invited guests either, but I couldn't help myself.

By the time we got to the front of the pie shop, whoever had been there was gone.

Grace looked miffed. "We missed them."

"Do you think there was more than one of them?" I asked her.

"No, I just meant that whoever was there managed to get away," she said as she looked up and down the avenue. "Should we keep looking?"

"Not unless you want to take a chance on being seen here

ourselves," I said. "Come on back out of view. There's something I want to check out."

Grace glanced at the police tape over the front door and shrugged. "I might as well, because it's clear we're not going to get inside this way."

She walked right past the overgrown bushes. Only when I stopped in my tracks did she hesitate. "Suzanne, what are you doing?"

"There's something behind those bushes," I said as I played the beam of light over what I'd seen earlier.

"I can't imagine what it might be," she said as she peered into the foliage as well.

Taking a deep breath, I worked my way into the living mass, hoping that the bushes at least weren't prickly and scratchy.

Unfortunately, that hope was in vain.

"Ouch," I said as a particularly vicious stem caught my arm. It had to have drawn blood, but I was committed. I had to see for myself if there really was a door there after all or if it was just a product of my overactive imagination.

"Would you come out of there before you hurt yourself?" Grace asked.

"Too late. I made it," I said. There was indeed a door hidden away from sight! How often it had been used in the past forty years, though, I couldn't say. The doorknob looked to be rusted, and most of the small window in the side of the frame was coated with dirt and grime. Only a small patch of glass level with the lock reflected any light at all. In fact, it looked as though it had recently been cleaned!

Taking an edge of my shirt, I tried the doorknob with little hope that it would open.

To my surprise, the door gave way easily.

One small step through the threshold, and I was inside the pie shop!

Man oh man, was it dark! I was glad I still had my flashlight. I was about to take another step into the darkness when I realized that Grace was still talking to me outside. Flashing my light around before I turned to leave, I took in my surroundings.

It felt as though I had somehow managed to sneak into some kind of coffin, the space was so tight and forbidding! I poked my head back outside just as she was finishing.

"...so I really think that's what we should do."

"I agree with you completely," I said. "Only I don't know what you just said. I was already inside the building. Are you coming?"

"I just said that I tried to get through too, but it was too hard without the light. Would you mind shining it my way so I can see how to get through that infernal scrub pile of bushes that are in the way?"

"Oh, I can do that," I said as I did as she suggested. "There, does that help?"

"Oh, yes. I can see you just fine now," a familiar man's voice said from outside the space I was currently in. "Come on back out, Suzanne. We need to have ourselves a little chat."

Evidently our visit to the pie shop hadn't gone completely unnoticed by the police after all unless the chief had just gotten lucky finding us there.

"Do I have to come back out through the bushes?" I asked. "I got scratched up pretty good coming in."

"Sorry, but I can't take a chance on you contaminating the crime scene any more than you already have," he said.

"But I took just one step inside, and I used my shirt to open the door so I wouldn't get any fingerprints on it," I protested.

"I'm willing to concede the point, but you could have

smudged any fingerprints that might have been there in the first place," he said. "Come on. Let's go. I don't have all night."

I heard some whispering, but there was really nothing else I could do. Taking a deep breath, I started back outside.

The chief of police must have been waiting for my light to start moving, because he suddenly called out, "Fine. We'll do it your way. Suzanne, you need to stay exactly where you are. I'm coming around to get you." Then he must have added to Grace, "As for you, you need to stay put, too."

Evidently my friend had pled my case with the police chief about providing me with an easier way out. I was happy I didn't have to go through that tangled mess again.

In less than a minute, I heard an outer door open, and then there were footsteps coming in my direction.

They passed right by me, though. "Chief, I'm in here."

"Where is here?" he asked, his voice muffled.

I reached out and knocked on the wall in front of me. "Does that help?"

One of the wall sections beside me moved after a few moments from what must have been a hard push. "You've got to be kidding me," he said when he shined his light into my eyes.

"Hey, would you mind lowering that thing? You are blinding me with it."

"That's what you get for sneaking around crime scenes in the middle of the night," he said, clearly trying to keep the chuckle out of his voice.

"It's hardly the middle of the night," I protested, since everything else he'd said had been true.

"It is for you," he countered.

"Okay, I'm guilty on all counts. Where exactly did I end up?" I asked as I followed him out of the coffin-sized space.

"It's really pretty cool. No wonder we missed it before.

Between the camouflage outside and the way it's hidden in here, I'm amazed anyone's seen it for years."

"That's the thing, though," I said as I studied the "door" he'd just pushed open. It was actually a large bookcase hinged on one side. As the chief demonstrated, it moved back and forth with a little effort on his part. I could see that when it was closed, it would be nearly impossible to tell that it concealed a door to the outside. "Someone knew about it, and recently. There's a smudge on the side window of the door about the height of the knob, and for something that looked pretty rusty when I first saw it, it appeared to me that someone had sprayed something on it recently to loosen it up."

"How did you even find it in the first place?" he asked, clearly admiring my discovery a bit.

"I got lucky," I admitted. "I would have never seen it in the light of day, but when my flashlight beam caught a reflection as Grace and I were chasing someone around the building, I knew that *something* was back there."

The police chief had been leading me out to the back door of the shop when he stopped suddenly in his tracks. "What did you just say?"

"Oh, I wouldn't put too much into it," I said. "It could have been a big dog or even a cat," I added, realizing how ridiculous it must have sounded. "You know how shadows are sometimes. They can be much bigger than what is producing them."

"Even if that's true, it would be hard to mistake an animal for a man," he said.

"Or a woman," I corrected him. It wasn't that I was taking some kind of stand for women's rights, though who could possibly object to that? If I'd learned anything over the years, it was that murder was an equal-opportunity crime.

"Or a woman," he agreed. "So, which was it?"

"Someone was out there," I said, realizing in retrospect that it was true. There was no way it could have been an animal unless the shadow caster had been walking around on two legs instead of the usual four, no matter what tricks the image might have been playing on us.

"And you two took off after them, on your own and without backup of any kind," he said, scolding me as he continued to escort me to the door. "Don't either one of you have any more sense than that, Suzanne?"

"You'd think so, but no, probably not," I said.

"I'm going to have to post someone inside the shop after all. One of my people isn't going to be getting any sleep tonight," he said as he led me out front. "I know just who the lucky winner is, too. Darby is going to be the perfect night watchman."

Darby Jones was one of Chief Grant's deputies, and I knew that he was still in the doghouse for a few things that had happened lately. I wanted to defend him, but something told me that I should stay out of police business, so for a complete change of pace, I kept my mouth shut.

Once we were back outside, Grace asked, "What took you so long?"

"There was a hidden doorway through a bookcase in the hallway," I blurted out.

"I don't suppose there's *any* chance you won't tell anyone *else* that, will you?" the chief of police asked sarcastically.

"Who else would I tell? Grace knows, Jake is out of town, and you were right there with me when the two of us figured it out," I said.

"Suzanne, knowing you as I do, the news will probably be spread all over town before I get back to my office," he said.

"I resent that remark," I said, not matching his joking tone of voice. I took my word seriously, and it was important that he knew that.

The chief pretended to mishear me. "I'm sorry, did you say that you resembled that remark?"

I looked in the light to see him smiling slightly and suddenly realized that I'd probably overreacted, especially given the circumstances. The man was having a hard time of it, both professionally and personally, and I certainly didn't need to add any to his troubles. "Maybe I should have," I said. "Okay, we'll both keep it quiet. We promise."

"Good. I'd appreciate that." The police chief locked the door as soon as we were back outside, made a quick call on his radio, and then he turned to Grace. "That pot pie was delicious. I'm just sorry I missed our dinner together."

It was a real olive branch, and I hoped that Grace didn't chide him for missing their planned shared meal. To my delight, if she had any misgivings at the moment, she was keeping them to herself. "It's fine. After all, we're doing it tomorrow night, right?"

"Right," he agreed before adding, "Unless there's a break in the case."

"Of course. That goes without saying," Grace said before turning to me. "Suzanne, are you ready to go?"

What I really wanted was to go back inside that building, but that was clearly off the table now. "I'm ready if you are." I turned back to the chief before returning to my Jeep. "Good night, Chief. It was nice seeing you."

"Good night," he said, watching us both as we got in and drove away.

"That went well, wouldn't you say?" Grace asked as she glanced back over her shoulder at her boyfriend, maybe once and future, at any rate.

"Well, I didn't get to snoop around inside, and we got

caught flatfooted, so no, I wouldn't say that it was particularly successful as far as an investigation is concerned," I said, a little miffed that we'd been caught so easily.

"Suzanne, you're missing the point here," Grace said.

"What, that you and Stephen are getting along better while you're breaking up than you ever did while you were dating?" I realized how snippy I must have sounded, and I felt instantly bad about it. "Strike that. I'm happy you two are at least communicating these days."

"I am too, but that's not what I meant," Grace explained. "I've got a hunch we just found out how the killer got into the pie shop without being seen. Just think. That means that there's a good chance that Leanne didn't do it! After all, with a secret way in and out of the building, *anyone* could have poisoned Maggie's meds."

"That's true," I admitted.

"Even if it makes our sleuthing a lot harder now, at least it should take some of the heat off of Leanne," she said.

"Probably. Blast it all, it just gets more and more complicated by the minute, doesn't it?" I asked as I pulled into Grace's driveway.

"Yes, but if we're going down, at least we're going to go down swinging," Grace answered as she got out, lingering a few moments before closing her door. "The thing is, whoever used that secret door now knows that we're onto them. If they thought they were being clever about it, they're going to figure out that we were too smart for them, and that makes us a real threat to them getting away with murder."

"Why does that not make me feel better right before going to sleep in a cottage all by myself?" I asked her with a smile.

"If you'd like, you can bunk with me here tonight," she said.

I considered taking her up on her offer, but my hours were so wildly different from hers that she'd be sitting around the place for hours while I slept. All in all, it wouldn't be much of a sleepover. "Thanks, but I'm good. I'll just double-deadbolt everything when I get back to the cottage, and I should be fine."

"Okay, if you're sure, but if you change your mind, remember, I'm just down the road."

"I'm counting on it," I said with a grin.

After she closed the Jeep door, I drove the rest of the way home. Jake had put a motion-sensitive light near the front porch for just such nights as tonight, but it had been on the fritz lately and didn't work all of the time. To my embarrassment, though no one else was there to see, I shut off the Jeep's engine, grabbed my keys, and raced up the steps to my front door.

As I did so, I slipped on the top step, banging my shin in the process. Scrambling inside, I was laughing about my own stupidity as I locked myself securely inside my own little fort.

I was going to have a nice bruise tomorrow, and possibly a limp as well to go along with a few scratches from the bushes I'd recently penetrated.

Oh well. It was the least I deserved for being so jumpy.

Then again, Grace had been right about one thing.

If word got out about our discovery of the secret door, and I was certain that it would somehow manage to before dawn, a killer would know that we were hot on their trail.

And that might be a very bad thing for us indeed.

Then again, it might mean that whoever had poisoned Maggie Moore might make a slip of their own, and if they did, Grace and I would be there to catch them red-handed.

CHAPTER 7

"**H**EY, JAKE. IT'S ME. No need to call me back. I'm just heading off to bed, and I thought I'd take a chance and call you. Sleep well, and I'll talk to you later. I love you. Bye." Even though we hadn't had a chance to chat before bed, I felt better just hearing his voice on his answering message, and leaving him something to remind him of how much I cared about him was just an added bonus.

I couldn't sleep in our bed, and after a solid forty-five minutes, I gave up, took my pillow and blanket out to the couch, and put on a YouTube channel that offered the background noise of rain pounding down on a tent. I wasn't a very big fan of camping, but there was something about that noise that soothed me, and before I knew it, I somehow managed to nod off.

I heard something, a sound of some sort, coming from the other room, and for a second, in my grogginess I thought it might be a smoke detector, but once I managed to come fully awake, I realized it was just the alarm I always set on my cell phone to make sure that I would wake up in time to make the donuts yet again. I hadn't really gotten enough sleep, but it was going to have to do. Time—and donuts—waited for no woman.

The air was finally starting to chill some at night as summer slowly lost its annual battle with autumn, and I grabbed a light sweater on the way out to ward off the chill, though I knew it would be hot enough later in the day. I got into the Jeep and drove the short distance to Donut Hearts, parking away from the door and making my way in. As I locked the door of the donut shop behind me, I went through my regular routine, flipping on the coffee pot and deep fryer as well as a few lights, but by no means all of them. I usually didn't mind working the first few hours by myself in silence, but with Emma gone, I decided I needed some music, so I tuned in to an oldies station. Though I had no idea where the station originated from, I was just happy that I was close enough to pick up its signal. Apparently it was an ABBA morning at the station, and I found myself working along with their greatest hits, something that was just fine with me. One of the real benefits of working by myself was being able to belt out the words along with the group. Alone, I had no qualms or hesitations about joining right in, even at times at the top of my lungs when I actually remembered the right words.

After the cake donuts were finished and the yeast dough was going through its first resting stage, I grabbed some coffee and headed outside, happily humming along with some of the music I'd just been listening to.

To my surprise though, when I locked the door, effectively blocking my way back in, I heard a man's voice coming from just behind me.

"Don't have any of that to spare, do you?" Darby Jones asked me sheepishly as he looked at my coffee cup.

"You scared the fool out of me," I said, something my grandmother used to say all of the time. "What are you doing sneaking around town in the middle of the night, Darby?"

"I've got sentry duty at the pie shop," he said with a frown. "As a matter of fact, I've been guarding it all night."

"Except for right now, you mean," I reminded him.

"Rick is taking the duty for a half hour so I can get something to eat. The only problem is that nothing's open this time of morning. I don't suppose you could let me buy some coffee from you before you are officially open, could you?"

The poor man looked so forlorn that I didn't have the heart to refuse him, not that I would have, anyway. "Come on in."

"I hate taking you away from your break," he said.

"You know about my schedule?" I asked, just a little bit creeped out that the cop would know when I took my breaks.

"Oh, yes. Usually you and Emma are out here together. I can see you from the top window of town hall if I look out the right window."

"What are you doing there so late at night?" I asked him, but then I realized that I already knew the answer. "You've been working more than your share of nights lately, haven't you?"

"I don't mind," he said, stifling a yawn. "Somebody's got to do it."

"But not every shift," I said. I grabbed a mug and filled it up, then said, "Excuse me for one second." Ducking into the kitchen, I put a fritter and a lemon-filled donut on a plate, two of Darby's favorites. As I slipped them in front of him, I said, "Sorry, but the bear claws aren't ready yet."

"I'm not about to be a choosy beggar. What do I owe you for these?"

"They're on the house, and so is the coffee."

He clouded over for a moment. "I'm afraid I can't do that. The chief has made himself pretty clear about us accepting *anything* free of charge from local merchants. A five should cover it, shouldn't it?"

"With change left over," I said, knowing better than to argue with him about it. Chief Grant was the one in the position where he made the rules, and his people would do well to follow them. I for one wasn't about to try to get them to do otherwise. I had a tenuous enough relationship with the man these days without adding to it.

"Keep it," he said as he took a long sip of coffee. "That's delightful. What's your secret?"

"Serve it hot, plain, and in abundance," I said with a grin. "Emma is usually in charge of our coffee selections, but I have pretty pedestrian tastes myself."

"I'm with you," Darby said, and then he took a bite of his lemon donut. "That's amazing. I love the filling."

"It's the best lemon curd I can find," I said. "I make it myself when I have the time, but lately I've had my hands full just running the place alone."

"Emma's coming back though someday, right?"

"That's the plan," I said. "Is the chief keeping you in his own personal doghouse because of what happened with Cassandra Lane?"

"My, this coffee is just what the doctor ordered," Darby said, clearly avoiding the question. I couldn't blame him. I knew there were times when I just wished everyone would leave me alone and let me enjoy my day, so why should the police officer be any different?

"I'm glad you like it," I said, taking another sip myself, dropping the subject altogether.

"Aren't you having a donut, too? I surely hate to eat alone."

"If I kept everyone company here while they ate, I wouldn't be able to fit through the front door," I said.

"Come on. One isn't going to hurt anything," he said with a wicked grin.

"Why not?" I asked. I grabbed a lemon-filled one for myself and rejoined him. Before I walked out of the kitchen though, I asked him, "Would you like another while I'm back here? You're entitled to at least one more."

"I'd love to, but I'd better not," he said. "I've got to be able to walk back to the pie shop, so I'd better stop while I still can."

"I understand," I said, taking a healthy bite of the donut. He was right. This lemon filling might just be better than the curd I normally made myself. If that was the case, I wasn't going to go to the trouble of making it anymore. I liked to offer the best ingredients I could, whether they came from my kitchen or someone else's. "Wow, this is so good it should almost be illegal."

"You can keep trying to entice me, but I'm not eating any more," Darby answered with a sigh. After finishing his treats and downing his coffee, he asked, "Could I get one of these to go, and maybe an old-fashioned donut, too?"

"Still feeling a little peckish?" I asked him as I did as he requested.

"No, these are for Rick. He did me a favor coming in, so I'd like to thank him for taking the trouble."

"And nothing says thank you like coffee and donuts, at least not as far as I'm concerned," I said with a smile.

"What do I owe you for the extra?"

"Would you believe your change covers it exactly?" I asked with a grin.

He took out two single dollar bills and put them on the counter. "Not a chance."

I didn't take the money, though. "I don't suppose you'd be willing to trade donuts and coffee for information, would you?"

"Suzanne, you know better than to even ask," he said. I was about to apologize for pushing him too far when he added, "For example, I couldn't tell you that the poisoned pills had been dipped in some bizarre chemical I'd never heard of until tonight."

"It surely wouldn't be vanalaxis macromium, would it?" I asked.

He looked surprised by my information. "No, it wouldn't be," Darby said as he nodded his head up and down. "Or that there were no fingerprints at all on the doorknob you discovered earlier."

"Oh, no. I didn't rub them off beyond recognition, did I?" It was hard enough staying out of the official investigation, but if I destroyed evidence that might prove valuable to them during my own searches, I'd never be able to forgive myself.

"No, that doorknob had been polished within an inch of its life," he said, raising his eyebrows to show that it was significant.

I got it instantly. Whoever had gone that way, either in or out, must have been up to no good. Why else do their best to cover their tracks? It was a clue provided by the absence of something, not its presence, like the dog that didn't bark in the night.

"Is there anything else that you're not allowed to tell me?" I asked him with a grin.

"No," he said, shaking his head in the negative to vouch for what he was saying. "That's all we've got so far."

"Well, don't keep me posted about anything else," I said, shaking my head up and down so vigorously I almost dislocated my neck.

He didn't answer in kind, only laughing as he left the donut shop. I was still thinking about where we stood in our unofficial investigation when my timer went off. I needed to get back to my yeast donuts, but that didn't mean I couldn't ponder everything I'd learned as I worked.

"Excuse me, miss. Can you help me?" a middle-aged man asked me as he studied my display cases full of donuts an hour after I'd opened for the day. I'd offered to wait on him twice during the ten minutes he'd been in Donut Hearts, but he'd steadfastly refused both times. I was more than happy to help him now, especially since he was blocking other people who apparently already knew what they wanted.

"I'd be delighted," I said. "What can I get you?"

"Well, the problem is that I don't see it here, but I'd know it if you'd just name the kinds of donuts you usually serve, I'd be able to come up with it," he said with a puzzled frown.

"Seriously? That would be quite a list," I said, looking at the four people standing behind him waiting in line.

"Oh, I've got loads of time. I don't mind," he said with a grin.

"Tell you what. Why don't you have a seat right over there and we can chat while I'm waiting on these other nice folks?" I thought it was a perfectly reasonable request, but apparently I was alone in my assumption.

"So, are you saying that you *won't* wait on me?" he asked as he started to cloud up.

"I'm not saying that at all," I said, doing my best to keep my voice level and even. Part of working with the public meant that I couldn't just spout off at someone who happened to annoy me, but some of my customers really pushed the limit. "If you could just tell me what you like, I'd be more than happy to serve you promptly and with a smile."

"Is it my fault that I can't remember what the bloody thing is called?" he asked me heatedly.

Well, yeah, kind of. "Tell you what. Let's see if we can't see to you right now. Is it a cake donut, or a yeast one?"

"What's the difference?" he asked.

Had this man ever even *had* a donut before in his life? I reached into one of the cases and pulled out one of each. "This is called a cake donut. It uses batter instead of dough, and its consistency is, well, for want of a better term, cakelike. You can use the basic recipe, or enhance the batter with lots of different flavors." I showed him the plain cake donut and broke it apart so he could see. Then I took the yeast donut and explained, "These are made from a dough, and they are light and airy compared to the cake donuts. They all have the same basic makeup, but they are either stuffed or iced with different flavors. Now, which one are you thinking of?"

"Is there a third choice?" he asked, and I saw Perry David roll his eyes dramatically, making a joke out of it, as was his habit with just about everything. I knew that there was an underlying truth to his protest, but Perry was just going to have to wait. I was on a mission now.

"Of course. We have apple fritters and bear claws and lots of yummy things like that," I said, pointing to where I usually stocked them. I had a few claws left, but a stranger had bought me out of fritters an hour earlier, which was always a mixed blessing. I loved making a big sale, but I hated disappointing customers who were looking for a special treat that I no longer had.

"Apple. That's it," he said. "I want one of those."

"I'm truly sorry, but we sold out earlier," I said, and he started to frown immediately. Before he could rant about how unprepared I was, I offered, "I have some apple-flavored donuts that I think you'll like. There are real apple pieces in the cake batter."

"I don't know. It's not the same, is it?"

I shrugged as I grabbed a donut anyway and put it on a napkin. "Try it. If you don't like it, it's on the house. Strike that. You don't have to pay for it even if you love it. How's that for a deal?"

"Okay. I guess it will do," he said a little glumly. Honestly, some people weren't even happy getting something for nothing. "How about something to drink?"

I quoted him the price for a cup of coffee, and it was clear he'd expected me to throw that in for free as well. "No, just the donut will be fine," he answered a little sullenly.

I put one of the apple donuts in a bag, not even asking him if he wanted to eat it there at the donut shop. The faster I could get this guy out of Donut Hearts, the better, as far as I was concerned. He didn't even seem to notice my conscious decision to keep him moving. Instead of taking the hint, he stayed right in his seat and promptly started eating the free donut, frowning with every bite. Sometimes you just couldn't win.

"Sorry about that, Perry," I said as the next customer approached the counter. "What can I get for you?"

Perry pretended to study the choices for a full ten seconds before he said, "I think an apple fritter sounds perfect."

I had to laugh, knowing the man as I did. He was usually good for a quick smile or a laugh, and I enjoyed having him around. "Fine," I said.

"I didn't think you had any fritters left," the man I'd turned down earlier said guardedly.

"That's because you didn't use the secret word," Perry said as he turned to him with a smile.

"Don't believe a word he tells you," I said. "I'm truly out of fritters. I was just going to offer him the same deal I gave to you. Surely you can't have a problem with that." I stared at him, my smile never wavering a bit.

"No, I suppose that's fine."

There were four more apple cake donuts left, so I grabbed the entire tray and pulled it out. "Who else wants to take me up on my one-time-only offer?"

Seven hands shot up. "Sorry, but it's first come, first served," I said. "I have only four left."

Perry looked pleased to be among the chosen few, but after he collected his free donut, he made a show of pulling out his wallet, extracting a five-dollar bill, and stuffing it into the tip jar. Then he smiled brightly at me as he added, "Thank you." I was about to protest his tip when he turned to the stranger and said, "By the way, 'thank you' is the secret word."

"Technically, that's two words," the stranger said with a frown.

I wasn't sure how Perry would react to the obvious scolding nature of the man's tone, but I surely wasn't expecting him to start laughing, loud and long. It was infectious, and soon everyone in the donut shop, with one notable exception, was laughing, too.

The man shoved the remnants of his free donut aside and headed for the door, but not before saying, "You are all stark raving mad."

"Don't we know it," Perry said, barely able to choke out the words from laughing so hard.

"Take your five back," I told him once the man was gone. "You made your point, which was greatly appreciated, I might add."

"Are you kidding? You earned every dime of that. I haven't laughed that hard in ages. See you tomorrow," he said before pausing at the door and adding, "I'm hoping you're out of apple fritters again."

"Not much chance of that happening," I said with a smile.

I managed to get through the rest of the morning with a smile thinking about what had happened, but that all ended ten minutes before I was due to close up for the day and take up my second job, amateur sleuthing.

And that was when trouble walked through the front door, whether I was ready for it or not.

CHAPTER 8

"I 'VE BEEN DOING SOME DIGGING on my own, Suzanne," Gabby Williams said as I spun around to face her. "Why are you here making donuts when my niece's freedom might be at stake?"

"Is the police chief focusing on her exclusively?" I asked Gabby. At least the shop was experiencing one of its all-too-frequent lulls, so we didn't have to keep our voices down.

"Not that I'm aware of. It's only a matter of time, though, isn't it? She was alone with Maggie when she died, so who else could it have been?"

"Is that what you came to tell me, that there's no one else we should even be *considering*?" I asked her. If that was her way of supporting Leanne, it wasn't a very good one.

"Of course not. Right now I've got three brand-*new* names for you to investigate, but that's going to be hard to do if you're standing around here making donuts and waiting on customers." She seemed to notice for the first time that we were alone in Donut Hearts. "By the way, where *are* all of your customers?"

"Beats me," I said as I wiped the countertop with a clean towel. "That's what I've been asking myself for the past six months."

"Don't worry, once the cool weather kicks in, they'll be back."

"Can you guarantee that?" I asked her. I'd won a decent sum with a scratch-off ticket earlier, but that money was nearly gone, and I couldn't count on Lady Luck to keep smiling down upon me. Things weren't dire just yet, but they were heading in that direction. What was it with people? Were they cutting out fattening treats altogether? What joy did that bring them in their lives? I counted on crowds of folks indulging themselves at least once in a while, but as things stood, that group now was barely a handful.

"Of course I can't, but it just stands to reason. After all, we're still in bathing-suit season. Not for me, of course, but for a lot of people."

Gabby was trim and neat in her stylish outfits, and it killed me that she would probably look better in a bathing suit than I would. "You know, you still have the figure to pull it off," I said.

My neighbor grinned for a split second before recapturing her composure. "What complete and utter nonsense. Now, do you want to hear these names or not?"

"By all means," I said, grabbing an order pad and a pen as a joke.

"Good. At least you are taking this seriously." Her approval made me smile, but I did my best to choke it back. In the process of doing that, I literally choked on my own saliva and started coughing for a few moments before I could get myself under control. Gabby looked at me with displeasure, and when I was finally able to stop, she tapped my pad. "The first person you should investigate is Crusty Lang, while the second needs to be Jane Preston."

"I've known Mrs. Preston forever, since she was my teacher in school, but I don't really know Crusty all that well," I said, failing to write either name down at the time. "Besides, why would either one of them poison Maggie?" Crusty was an undersized fellow, a confirmed bachelor who liked to think of himself as a ladies' man. He'd flirt with any female from twenty to sixty, which, even at the highest end of the scale, was still younger than he was.

"Let's take Crusty first. He and my cousin had a tryst last month, and he wasn't at all happy when Maggie ended it," Gabby said archly.

"Hang on a second. You're telling me that the bantam rooster was thinking about settling down?" That's what we called Crusty, at least behind his back. He was just like a bantam, small in size but extra large in ego and bravado. With a shock of yellowish-white hair much like a rooster's comb atop his head, Crusty's arrogant strut made the comparison even more noticeable.

"You'd be amazed by the scope of men Maggie attracted, despite her rather unpleasant demeanor at times," Gabby said. "Suzanne, why aren't you writing any of this down?"

I took a few quick notes, as though there was any chance I could ever wipe the image of Crusty and Maggie out of my mind, and then I turned back to Gabby.

"Got it. Now what about Mrs. Preston?" Jane Preston was a retired schoolteacher and just about as sweet a woman as you'd ever want to meet. "Why should *she* have an issue with Maggie?"

"Didn't you know? Dear, you really must get out of this shop every now and then, or life is going to pass you by."

"I'll see what I can do about that, but in the meantime, what about Mrs. Preston? What possible reason could she have to kill Maggie?"

"Clearly more than you realize. It appears that the two women were rivals for Crusty's affection," she said smugly.

"I don't believe it," I said, shaking my head so hard it rattled my teeth. There was no way I could see Jane enamored with that cocky little man. I hadn't even realized she'd dated anyone after her husband had passed away the year before.

"It's true enough, and if you don't believe me, you can ask her yourself," Gabby said before looking at her watch. "Why don't you close the donut shop early? No one else is coming in, anyway," she added.

"Thanks for the vote of confidence," I said just as a group of six people in their mid-twenties came into Donut Hearts, thankfully disproving Gabby's dire prediction.

One particularly happy man waved a twenty-dollar bill in the air. "Donuts for my friends, and fresh water for our horses."

"Wayne, stop it. This lady is going to think you're crazy," one of the women said with a laugh.

"Hey, as long as you're buying donuts for everyone, I'll think anything you'd like me to," I said with a grin.

"This, my friends, is a woman after my own heart," the young man said.

"What exactly are we celebrating?" I asked him, happy to have their glowing enthusiasm in my shop. The place had been somber enough lately.

"I just got engaged," he said proudly.

I looked at the three women with him. "Excellent. Which one of you deserves my congratulations?" I asked them happily.

"Suzanne, you are *never* supposed to congratulate a bride," Gabby said dismissively. "You wish her well."

"Either way, she's not here, thank goodness, so it really doesn't matter," one of the girls replied.

"Where is the lucky lady, if I may ask?" I wondered aloud.

"She's overseas studying at the moment, but she's coming back home to me next week," the groom-to-be said. "My dear lady, you may feel free to congratulate *me*."

"I'll do better than that. The donuts and the fresh water are on the house."

That brought whoops of delight from the group, while

Gabby said, "Suzanne, it's no wonder you're in financial trouble. You can't just keep giving your food away."

"Whether I do or not, it's my business, Gabby, and I mean that quite literally." I smiled, but I made sure she saw that there was an edge of steel in my gaze. I meant it. Until I had to lock the doors and shut down for good, I would continue to run Donut Hearts as *I* saw fit, and no one was going to stop me from doing it.

"As much as I appreciate the offer, I insist on paying," the young man said with a happy smile. "Pick out your finest treats, and keep the change with our compliments for joining us in our celebration."

"You're really giddy, aren't you, Wayne?" one of the guys asked him.

"Wouldn't you be? Did any of you ever think for one second that Cynthia would say yes? Come on; don't be shy. I'm just as surprised as the rest of you!"

Gabby harrumphed once, and then she exited, which made them smile even brighter, and once she was gone and safely away, their laughter cut loose.

All in all, it was a really neat way to end the workday.

Once they were on their way, I found myself smiling. Cynthia was no fool. Wayne loved her, that much was clear, and I had a hunch that he'd spend the rest of his life doing his utmost to make her happy. If you asked me, the world needed more men and women like that.

It was finally time to lock the doors, but just as I was about to, Grace ran up and slid in just in time. "Hang on. I'm here," she said a little breathlessly.

"There's no rush. I have a pile of dishes to do, I need to sweep the kitchen and the dining area, balance the register, and complete half a dozen other tasks before we can go. Don't worry, I won't even ask you to pitch in."

"Then I will do so gladly," Grace said with glee. She'd already changed from her business suit to a stylish knit dress that showed off her figure. I kind of wished the police chief would wander by. If he could see what he was about to throw away, he might not be so eager to jettison her. "I feel like doing some dishes. After all, I've been told that it can be very therapeutic." I'd used that line to convince her to do dishes before, and in her defense, she'd pitched in then as well.

"Well, I won't say no," I told her. "I could really use the help."

As we started cleaning up together, she asked me, "When is Emma coming back?"

"Soon, I hope," I told her.

"You don't even know?"

"We kind of left her return open-ended," I admitted. "After all, if she's not working, I don't have to pay her. Besides, I'm willing to bet that she and Sharon are having a lovely time, no matter where they ended up."

Grace had offered to chip in and help me through my current dry spell, but I couldn't take her up on it any more than I could have taken money from my mother. I was going to weather this alone, or at least with Jake, one way or the other.

"Got it," Grace said. "Well, don't just stand there. Get busy, woman. We have people to interview."

"More than you even know," I said, briefing her on Crusty and Mrs. Preston as I worked.

She was just as surprised as I had been, especially about our former teacher. "You just never know, do you?"

"The truth is I still don't. Until I hear the words coming out of her mouth, I'm not going to be able to believe it."

"Then I suggest we hustle and get this work finished so we can go ask her ourselves," Grace said.

Twenty minutes later, the books were balanced, the last of

the dishes were finished, and the donut shop was clean. I had four dozen donuts left over, usually something that would cause me great sorrow, but we were going to need them this afternoon in the course of our investigation. Everyone we called on was going to receive a free dozen donuts just for having the pleasure of speaking with us. I just hoped that Crusty, Mrs. Preston, Ashton, and Beatrice would appreciate the gesture and open up to us.

CHAPTER 9

A S WE WERE LOADING THE four stuffed boxes of donuts into the back of my Jeep, I asked Grace, "Any thoughts on who we should speak with first?"

"Well, part of me says we should find the two folks in April Springs, since we can check them off our list pretty quickly, but the other part says we do our driving first and then wrap things up once we're back here."

"What's the breakdown on your preference?" I asked her.

"As far as I'm concerned, it's six of one and six of the other," she said with a smile. "I refuse to make a 'dozen' joke when we're serving as a pastry wagon."

"Don't you approve of my preferred method of bribery?" I asked her as I secured the last box in place. It wouldn't do to have them shift around and spill donuts in the back of my vehicle before we were able to deliver them.

"Not me. I'm all for it," Grace said. "How much credence can we put into the leads that Gabby gave you earlier?"

"Like always, I need to speak with these folks myself to see if I think they need to be added to our list of current suspects. Maggie had a rare talent for offending just about everyone she ever came into contact with, so *nothing* would surprise me at this point, except maybe if Mrs. Preston really was interested in Crusty. That would be a stretch of the imagination that I can't bring myself to cope with."

"I have an idea. I just realized something. There's a bonus

if we go see Beatrice first," Grace said with a sly grin. "She's in Union Square, at least as far as I was able to determine earlier."

"That certainly gives us a good place to start," I answered.

"And who else do we know in Union Square, someone who might be appropriate to see during lunchtime hours?" she asked as her smile widened.

"Trust me, you don't have to twist my arm to go to Napoli's," I said. The DeAngelis women, both mother and daughters alike, were amazing, and not just as culinary geniuses. They were also some of the nicest, most genuine folks I knew, besides being beautiful beyond comprehension.

"I didn't think so," Grace replied.

"Okay, but only on one condition; we need to see Beatrice first," I said. "Otherwise we might never get around to her if we're so stuffed we can barely move."

Grace reluctantly agreed. "That sounds like a solid plan to me," she said as we passed the future pie shop, the police station and jail, then St. Theresa's after finally heading the rest of the way down Viewmont Avenue toward Union Square.

"Beatrice has got to be near the top of our list, since she's the only one we know with *double* motives to want to see Maggie dead," I said.

"That's not entirely true though, is it?" Grace asked softly.

I realized immediately what she meant. "You're right. Leanne has two motives as well: the pie shop arrangement and the cookbook Maggie may or may not have stolen from her. I need to keep reminding myself that we need to keep her in mind as a suspect. Goodness, she should probably be our primary one. I'm sure Chief Grant believes that." I purposefully mentioned Grace's boyfriend by his title, just as a reminder that no matter what their personal relationship status was, he was still officially in charge of Maggie Moore's murder investigation.

"We might want to look into *her* life as well when we get

a chance," Grace said. "Suzanne, since Beatrice was Maggie's former sister-in-law, and she believes that her brother died under mysterious circumstances, could we be official investigators from Poison Control when we speak with her?" Grace asked me. She loved role-playing during the course of our investigations, but I was afraid that wasn't going to work this time.

"I'm not sure that would work. After all, wouldn't we need some kind of official identification badges to show her? I'm afraid dummying something up would eat up some of our valuable time, not to mention the fact that it's probably illegal impersonating government employees like that."

"Only if we get caught," Grace said with a smile. After a moment, she added, "I'm kidding, Suzanne!"

"Are you? Are you really?" I asked, risking a glance in her direction as I drove.

"For the sake of argument, let's say that I am," she answered. "If my research is correct, she'll be at Henri's, an upscale women's clothing store just off the downtown shopping district." Grace glanced at me, and then she added, "No offense, but maybe I should pretend to be a customer so we can question her."

I looked down at my jeans and T-shirt, and then I studied Grace's stylish dress. "Maybe you've got a point. Besides, how could I possibly be offended by that?" After I said it, I stuck my tongue out at her to show her that I was teasing right back. No one, and I mean no one, would ever confuse Grace's style with mine. The fact that each of us took great pride in that fact just made our bond that much stronger.

"Can I at least be your socially awkward friend?" I asked her.

"Isn't that your description already?" she asked with a perfectly innocent expression.

We both burst out laughing. It really had been quite amusing, but soon enough, we were pulling into a parking space in front of Henri's. I was happy Grace was taking the lead. I couldn't have felt more out of place if we'd just pulled up to a biker bar. Well, maybe it wasn't that bad, but it was still going to be a place where I would probably need an interpreter to follow along, given the fact that I didn't speak high fashion, or medium fashion, either.

"Hello, my name is Millicent. May I help you?" a petite young woman with doe eyes and barely into her twenties asked as she approached Grace. The saleswoman barely glanced sideways at me, even with my box of donuts, so I was glad I'd been prepared for the snub. Hey, I'd seen *Pretty Woman*. For all this woman knew, I was loaded with cash and ready to spend it, even though that was clearly not the case. Then again, she had no way of knowing that. I was tempted to charge a few thousand dollars' worth of clothes on my credit card just to prove to her that I could afford it. That thought made me smile, and I quickly abandoned the plan to show her that she'd misjudged me, even though clearly she hadn't.

I was saved from my foolishness when Grace spoke up for the two of us. "I'm afraid you won't do at all," she said, frowning at the young woman as though she were flawed in some way.

"Excuse me?" Millicent asked, clearly unhappy with Grace's assessment of her suitability to even wait on us.

"It's not you, dear. It's just that a friend recommended Beatrice. Is she here today, by any chance?"

The young woman nodded and frowned at the same time. It was clear that she didn't approve of our choice, and her next words simply confirmed it. "I hadn't realized you were looking for more of a *matronly* look," the young woman said, making sure to dig in the slam with extra emphasis.

"Honestly, it has been my experience that refinement *has* no age limits," Grace said, and then she held the woman's stare for much longer than I could have managed.

"Of course. Let me get her for you," Millicent said contritely.

Once she was gone, I asked Grace, "How did you do that?"

"Do what?" she asked me as she glanced through a few items of clothing on display. It struck me that though I wouldn't be caught dead in a shop like this one, Grace was clearly at home and fully at ease there. We really did run in different circles these days.

"You put her in her place so eloquently," I said. "Kudos on the brevity of language as well."

"Suzanne, deep down, nearly *all* of us think of ourselves as being unworthy. When someone else points it out, it merely reinforces our own self-image."

"Do *you* feel that way?" I asked her. "Because I surely don't."

"That's one of the things I love most about you," Grace said with a smile.

"I'm Beatrice," a woman in her late thirties said as she joined us. She was trim and stylish, but she looked to be a little tired of her job. Though the weather was quite warm, she wore a long-sleeved blouse that covered her arms to the wrists.

"Would you care for some donuts?" I asked her as I offered her the box.

She declined, looking at my treats as though they were radioactive. "I understand you requested me. Might I ask who recommended me?"

Was she asking to thank them or give them a kickback for steering us her way? Either way, I was surprised by Grace's answer, though not nearly as much as Beatrice was. "Maggie Moore told us all about you just before she died."

Beatrice's eyes immediately narrowed. "Now I know you're lying.

That woman wouldn't recommend me to anyone if I was the only one with a bucket of water and they were on fire."

"So then you're probably not all that unhappy that she's dead," I said.

Beatrice looked from Grace to me and then back again. "I'm sorry, but I was under the impression that you were interested in updating your wardrobe," she told Grace, trying to put her in her place for having the audacity to bring up something as distasteful as her late sister-in-law's recent murder.

Clearly Beatrice didn't know who she was messing with, though. "I should be the one apologizing. I'm truly sorry. I was under the impression that you sold clothes here. Can you really afford to let a commission just walk right out of the store, or worse yet, go to Millicent instead of you?" That last bit struck home, as it wasn't hard to see that the two women were rivals.

"How can I even be certain you're going to buy anything?" she asked Grace.

"That's the beauty of it; you can't," Grace replied. "Whether or not I shop here will depend on your answers. It's up to you, but we don't have all day."

It took Beatrice less than two seconds to make up her mind, and in the end, greed won out, which was often the case. "What do you want to know?" she asked wearily, conceding the point, game, set, and match.

It was a fair question at that. When exactly had Maggie's pills been tainted with poison? Without knowing that, the murder could have technically happened any time in the past several weeks, or at least the wheels could have been set in motion, if Maggie had been lucky in her pill Russian roulette. Then again, that doorknob at the pie shop had been freshly wiped of prints. Maybe that was the way to go. "When was the last time you were in April Springs?" I asked her.

Beatrice glanced over at me, sized me up in an instant as

someone who would *never* be a customer of hers, and then turned back to Grace.

"She asked you a question," Grace had the style to say.

"I was there last week," she reluctantly admitted as she glanced in my direction for a moment. "I heard that Maggie was opening a pie shop, and I knew for a fact that the woman couldn't boil an egg, let alone make an entire pie. Not an edible one, at any rate. I had to see for myself. I never spoke with her, though. She was nowhere to be found when I got into town, so I left without achieving my goal. I don't know what you've heard, but Maggie Moore was a horrid woman, and although I didn't kill her, I find it oddly fitting that she died the same way my brother did."

"Exactly how much was she set to inherit from his estate?" Grace asked.

Beatrice looked at Grace as though she'd just slapped her. "How do you know about that? It was supposed to be confidential."

"You know how these things are," Grace said with a wave of her hand. "Sometimes people talk. Well, what was her portion supposed to be?"

"Half his estate, which amounts to something around two hundred thousand dollars," Beatrice reluctantly admitted.

"That's more than enough motive for murder, not even mentioning the fact that she might have killed your brother," I said.

The saleswoman surely noticed me now! "She poisoned him, and because of the incompetence of the police, she was going to inherit half his wealth? I don't think so. It wasn't fair, but I wasn't going to just roll over and give it to her. I was going to contest it in court, no matter what the cost!"

"Even at your wages here?" Grace asked. "I'm guessing you can't touch your portion either until everything is settled."

"I'd rather die than give her a dime of Clifford's money," Beatrice said.

"Or kill Maggie to keep her from it," I added.

Beatrice looked at me with raw fury in her blazing stare. Before she could say anything else, she caught herself, spun around, and hurried away into the back room.

"Sorry about that," I said before Millicent could rejoin us.

"You don't have to apologize to me. It's all fine and dandy," Grace said.

"I'm sorry, but apparently Beatrice has been taken ill," Millicent said softly as she approached us. Was she actually smiling? "However, I'd be more than happy to wait on you myself." The gleam in her eyes testified to that.

"No, I believe we'll come back when she's feeling better," Grace said, leading me out of the store as Millicent continued to dog our steps.

Once we were outside, Grace said, "I don't know about you, but I'm ready for that lunch."

As we headed to Napoli's, I said, "Does Beatrice seem like someone willing to wait until Maggie took that poison?"

"She certainly hated her enough," Grace said.

"That's clearly true, but when you think about it, she had a pretty hard deadline, by her own admission. If Maggie managed to keep skipping the poisoned pills, she could have inherited her ex-husband's money before she took the first tainted one."

"Beatrice said that she'd fight it in court, though," Grace reminded me. "It's hard to tell how long it would all drag out before there was a final decision."

"That's what she told us, but I can't imagine her having enough cash reserves for any kind of legal battle."

"No, neither can I," Grace said. "But we still can't mark her off our list. She's such a good candidate, I just can't bring myself to do it."

"Neither can I. I'm not even sure we can put her on the back burner, even if we do have a handful of other suspects who might have been able to take a more leisurely approach to murder than Beatrice could afford to."

"You're right about that," Grace replied.

"I think we need to keep looking, don't you?"

"Yes, but *after* lunch, right?" Grace asked with a smile.

"Yes, after lunch," I agreed. I too was hungry for some of the DeAngelis fine cooking.

"What do we do with these, since no one at Henri's wanted them?" Grace asked as she tapped the box in my hands.

"We could always give them to the DeAngelis women," I said. "After all, at least *they* love my donuts."

"Suzanne, no one with the least bit of sense would *ever* turn your treats down," she said.

That made me feel a little better, but I still didn't like Beatrice Branch. Whether it was because of her refusal of my treats or the cavalier way she'd dismissed me, I honestly couldn't say.

CHAPTER 10

"CLOSED? HOW CAN THEY BE closed?" Grace asked as she rattled the front door of the restaurant.

"I don't understand it, either," I said. The posted hours for Napoli's were on the side window, and based on what it said, the Italian restaurant surely should have been open.

"Are they shut down just for today, or forever?" Grace asked me, clearly upset by what we'd found.

"There's just one way to find out," I said, pulling out my cell phone and calling Angelica DeAngelis directly.

My call went straight to voicemail though, and when I tried to leave a message, I was informed by a computer-generated voice that the mailbox was full. It thanked me for calling, but I doubted its electronic sincerity. "She didn't pick up," I said.

"This is possibly the worst day of my life," Grace said, grossly over exaggerating the situation. After all, we'd dealt with more than our fair share of killers in the past—and the aftermath they'd left behind their nefarious actions—and though I loved the food and company at Napoli's, there was such a thing as perspective.

"I've got one more idea," I said.

"Well, I'm too hungry to drive back to April Springs," Grace said with a pout.

"Get in the Jeep," I instructed her.

"You're not dragging me to Go Eats, are you?" she asked with disdain. The place had started off being called Good Eats a thousand years ago, but the second "o" and the "d" had fallen off, and the owner was too cheap to replace them.

"Not if we can help it, though even you have to admit that the last time we ate there, it wasn't nearly as bad as we thought it was going to be."

Grace frowned at me. "That's the expectation I always have when I eat out, for the food not to be quite as horrible as my already low expectations."

I smiled at her in spite of her mood. "You get grumpy when you're hungry. Did you realize that?"

"I'm *never* grumpy," she said with an exaggerated frown before breaking out into a broad smile. "Okay, maybe sometimes a little bit."

We drove around the strip mall where the restaurant was located, and I was relieved to see three cars parked behind Napoli's. "We're here."

"Hey, why are there cars here if they are closed?" Grace asked me.

"I don't know, but we're about to find out."

It took a pretty strong series of knocks before anyone answered the back door of the restaurant. "This had better be import..." Angelica said with a scowl until she realized that it was us. "Ladies," she added, her smile coming through bright enough to lighten the gloomiest day, "how lovely to see you. What a pleasant surprise."

While I might be considered cute on my best days, I couldn't touch the spark of beauty that lay within the DeAngelis women. In a way I felt sorry for Angelica's daughters. Even though they were all lovely in their own ways, their mother outshone them all. I had hoped that Angelica and George Morris might get together someday, and I had a hunch that the senior DeAngelis felt the same way, but so far George hadn't picked up on the hints we'd been dropping. Now that he was single again, albeit for the most tragic of reasons, I had hopes that he might pursue Angelica, because if anything, the woman was more beautiful on the inside than she was on the exterior, and that was saying something.

"You're closed," Grace told her in almost accusatory fashion. "How can that be? It's not permanent, is it?"

"Of course it's not," Angelica said, and then she turned to her youngest daughter, Sophia. "Dearest daughter, what did you say on the sign out front?"

"That we were closed, just like you told me," Sophia said, narrowing her gaze at her mother. "Don't tell me I managed to mess that up, too."

Evidently the women were battling about something, but I wasn't about to inquire what it might be. "I didn't mean to start anything," I said apologetically.

"Please, we've been having this exact same argument since I was old enough to cook," Sophia said, still staring down her mother.

"Perhaps it's because you don't listen, and you'd rather do things your way than anyone else's. Deny it if you dare."

"Are you kidding? Mom, I embrace it," Sophia said with a wicked little smile.

"You do?" Her daughter's reaction clearly took her by surprise.

"Of course. After all, I'm exactly like you."

Angelica was stunned by the statement, but before she could answer, one of Sophia's sisters, Antonia, said, "Way to go, Soph. She didn't see that one coming."

"Sweet," Maria added.

"Where's Tianna?" I asked, naming the missing sister as I looked around the kitchen.

"She's in Italy," Maria explained.

"Where we will all be joining her tomorrow," Sophia added.

"*If* we finish here in time, which is by no means certain at the rate we're going," Angelica added.

"You're going away?" I asked, hoping beyond hope that this was just a vacation and not something more permanent.

"I want the girls to see where they come from," Angelica answered.

"I come from Union Square," Sophia said with a grin.

"If you aren't interested in going with us, Sophia, you're more than welcome to stay here while the rest of us go," Angelica said.

Sophia approached her mother, hugged her, and then she said, "You'd miss me if I didn't go with you. Admit it."

"I never claimed otherwise," she said with a smile. "Now let me go, girl. We have work to do."

"How long will you be gone?" I asked Angelica.

"Two glorious weeks," she replied before turning back to Sophia. "Did you put that on the sign as well?"

"That part might have slipped my mind," she said as she grabbed a marker and headed out the door.

"That girl would forget her head if it weren't attached," Angelica said with a grin. I knew that she loved all of her daughters equally, but perhaps, just perhaps, Sophia held a special place in her heart.

"We'll miss you, but we hope you have a good time," I said as I started for the back door. It was clear they had more to deal with than feeding us, even though lovely smells surrounded them. The ladies must have been cleaning out their fridge before they left, but my oh my, the aromas coming from that stovetop were enough to break a woman's heart.

"Where are you rushing off to in such a hurry?" Angelica asked.

"We don't want to get in the way," Grace replied, though she was clearly as taken with the aromas of goodness as I was.

"Nonsense. We have more food here than we could ever eat, and any leftovers will just have to be thrown out. You aren't going to make me do that, are you?" she asked severely. Angelica felt the way I did about wasting food. It was to be avoided at all costs if at all possible.

That gave me an idea. "We'll eat with you on one condition," I said. Grace shot me a withering look, but I refused to budge.

"You are *not* going to pay for your meal," Angelica said firmly. "I would rather throw it all in the dumpster than take your money for something offered out of friendship."

Angelica was bluffing, and what was more, we both knew it, but that hadn't been my condition at all. "I'll trade you two meals for a box of donuts I have in my Jeep."

"That's not a fair trade at all," Angelica said.

"Okay, I can probably give you two boxes, but that's my final offer," I answered with a grin.

"I meant that we aren't bartering here. I'm asking you two to be my guests."

"And I'm trying to give you something as well. Surely you don't want to offend me any more than I want to show you disrespect," I replied.

We stayed that way, stare for stare, for what felt like forever but was most likely not more than sixty seconds. Still, a full minute of intense silence could seem like a very long time.

Finally, it was Maria who broke the logjam. She whooped with laughter as she clapped her hands. "Mom, I believe we found someone as stubborn as you."

"What about Sophia?" Angelica asked, her intense gaze loosening up a bit.

"Oh, she's a mere amateur compared to the two of you," Antonia answered.

"Should I be offended by that?" I asked Angelica.

"No, quite the contrary. Coming from my girls, it's the highest compliment they could possibly give you. Very well. I accept your offer."

"Two boxes of donuts for two meals?"

"One," Angelica said firmly.

"Eighteen, and that's my final offer," I said, laughing when I was unable to hold my position without letting my enjoyment of the situation slip out.

"It's a deal," she said, joining in my amusement as well as she stuck out her hand.

"I'll be right back," I said as I took it.

"The transaction can surely wait until after you eat," Angelica said, as Grace was starting to sit down at the table in the kitchen reserved for family and only the closest friends. It had been my honor and privilege to eat there many times in the past, and I hoped it would be again in the future.

"Come on, Suzanne. Everything smells wonderful," Grace pled, but the girls had been right. In my own way, I was just as stubborn as Angelica was, but then again, like them, I'd had an excellent teacher of my own. I had a fair chance of going up against Angelica, but with my mother, it was another thing altogether. That woman could out-stubborn a rock if ever the need arose, and I was painfully aware of it.

"I'll just be a second," I said as I walked out the back door to my Jeep. We still had our original four dozen donuts that we'd left April Springs with, but since Beatrice had rejected my generous offer, I now had enough to spare. Taking two donuts each from three of the boxes, I found a way to cram all eighteen into the remaining one. They looked a little worse for the wear being shoved in all together like that, but I didn't have any spare boxes on hand, and a deal was a deal, especially one I'd fought so hard to get.

"The box is a little too full," I apologized as I extended it to Angelica upon my return.

"I'll see if I can help make the situation better," Sophia answered, now back in the kitchen with everyone else. She took a cherry-iced yeast donut and then handed the box to her sisters. "Come on. Dig in. This is a rare treat for us."

"I can't believe you'd rather have my donuts than your own delicious cooking," I said in true wonder and astonishment.

"Think of it this way," Maria answered as she took a chocolate-iced-and-sprinkled cake donut for herself. "We can have our food any time we want. Your donuts are a real treat."

Antonia nodded with enthusiasm as she selected an old-fashioned cake donut, one of the plainest ones I served. "Plus, we didn't have to make these. How about you, Mom? Aren't you having one yourself?"

"I was just waiting for you all to get your first choices," Angelica said. She peered into the box, and I nearly apologized for the limited offering when she smiled brightly. "Is this cream filled? I love these donuts!"

"It is," I admitted, still shaking my head in wonder. "Now that I've kept my end of the bargain, I expect you to feed me in turn," I said with a grin.

"Just as soon as I have another bite," Angelica said, savoring my treat almost as much as I was about to enjoy hers.

"You go ahead and finish your donut, Mom. I'll take care of Grace and Suzanne," Sophia said, washing her hands in the sink and drying them on a nearby towel.

"Did you finish your treat *already*?" Angelica asked her.

"Hey, I'm a growing girl. I need as many calories as I can get," she said with a grin, sticking her tongue out at her sisters, who were both starting to round off a bit to look more and more like their mother. These three daughters might just be heading toward their mother's level of beauty after all. There was something to be said for Angelica's mature loveliness, a rounding and a softening of edges that most of us don't have in our youth. For me, I felt as though I just looked a little squishier, but for these three young women, they were, if anything, developing a new and deeper beauty that their youth had not been able to produce.

"I really don't mind," Angelica said, starting to put her donut down so she could serve us.

All three young women protested. "Mom, take a minute and enjoy the moment, okay? Isn't that what you're always telling us?" Antonia asked.

Angelica laughed as Sophia began to load our plates. "It's a terrible thing to have your own wisdom thrown back at you," she said with a grin, though it was clearly not so terrible at all. After examining the plates her youngest daughter had prepared for us, Angelica nodded in approval. "Well done, Sophia."

"Thank you kindly," she said with a half curtsy. "After all, I learned from the best. As a matter of fact, we all did."

As Grace and I began to tackle more food on just one of our plates than either one of us could eat, I asked Angelica, "Tell us about your trip."

By the time the meal was over, we'd been given a full itinerary of their planned travels, and I found myself wishing for an opportunity to go overseas again. Jake and I had honeymooned in Paris, and it had been wonderful, but there was so much more I longed to see there. Maybe, if things ever turned around at Donut Hearts and I actually started making a decent profit again, we could go back. That was an awfully big maybe.

After hugging all four of the women good-bye, Grace and I headed out to the Jeep so we could be on our way again.

"I don't know about you, but after that meal, I need a nap," I told her as I felt the seat belt straining across my waist.

"That sounds great, but sadly, we have work to do. At least we have an hour's drive ahead of us to recover, though I might nod off along the way, if you don't mind."

"Tell you what. I'll join you," I said with a grin.

"Perhaps that's not the *best* plan," she replied. "I'll make a deal with you. If you can manage to get us back to April Springs, I'll finish up the drive and get us to Maple Hollow."

"I might just take you up on that," I said as I started the drive.

Three minutes later, I was about to say something to Grace about the case we were investigating when I glanced over and saw that she was sleeping soundly.

At least one of us was getting some rest, and who knew? By the time we got to April Springs, I might just have to take her up on her offer to drive to Maple Hollow.

After all, it wasn't fair that she was the only one who got to take a snooze along the way, and she'd been right about something else, too.

We still had a great deal of work ahead of us if we were going to solve Maggie Moore's murder.

CHAPTER 11

"WHERE ARE WE?" GRACE ASKED me quite a bit later as she finally stirred in her seat. I loved my Jeep, but it wasn't the most comfortable ride in the world, and yet somehow Grace had managed to sleep for nearly an hour.

"We're just pulling into Maple Hollow," I said with a smile.

"I thought you were going to wake me up," she protested rather weakly.

"I considered it, but you were sleeping too soundly," I answered. "Besides, I wasn't in any danger of falling asleep. Your snoring made certain of that," I said as I laughed.

"At least let me drive back," she asked.

"We'll see. In the meantime, let's go have a chat with Ashton Belle. At least we know where to find him," I added as I pulled into the bank parking lot.

"*If* he's in," Grace said.

"Where else would he be on a workday at two in the afternoon?" I asked her.

"You never know."

Fortunately, we could see the man we were looking for through a large window in his office, seated at his desk and leafing through some paperwork. "Mr. Belle, these two ladies would like to see you," his assistant said as she led us into his private workspace.

"They brought you donuts," she added with a bright smile. The woman seemed happier about that prospect than she probably should have been.

"Put them in the break room, Stella, if you wouldn't mind," he said before he even looked up at us. Ashton looked a little distracted for a moment, but the expression was soon replaced by a steady and clearly artificial smile when he finally focused on us. "Thank you for your kind gesture. Now, what can I do for you ladies?"

"We're here about Maggie Moore," Grace said, brushing aside all pretense of subtlety.

"What about her?" he asked as his smile instantly vanished at the mention of the woman's name. "I'm not doing any more business with her until she drops her ridiculous claim that I owe her eight dollars. If she thinks sending two of her goons to my office is going to bully me into refunding a fee she clearly owed, she's sadly mistaken."

I looked at him and laughed, despite his serious tone. "You're kidding, right?"

"What's so funny?" he asked, suspicious that we were mocking him, because Grace had joined in as well. "Eight dollars might not seem like a great deal of money, but the fee was incurred, and it has to be paid."

"Do you actually think we're here on Maggie Moore's behalf, and what's more, that we're her *goons*?" Grace asked with a grin. "I've been called many things in my life, but never a goon."

"You know what I mean," he said brusquely, not finding our amusement enjoyable in any way, shape, or form. "Tell her I personally said for her to go bark at the moon. I'm finished with that woman, and that's that."

"More than you realize," I said, my earlier delight now gone.

"And why is that?" he asked me sternly.

"Because Maggie is dead," I said. "Someone poisoned her yesterday."

Ashton Belle shook his head with mild irritation. "I'm sorry, but I don't find your brand of humor amusing at all. I've been at a conference in San Francisco for eight days, and I just got back into town this morning. I'm jetlagged and sleep deprived, so if you'll excuse me, I've got real work to do."

"It's true. She's really dead," Grace said.

Ashton looked from Grace to me and then back at her again. "I find that difficult to believe."

"So did we, but it is the police's official opinion, and we agree. Someone poisoned her."

"Well, I certainly didn't do it," he said gruffly. "I suppose I have the perfect alibi, since I can prove that I've been out of town for the past week."

"You'd think so, wouldn't you?" I asked him.

"Yes I would, but the implication is that you think I'm wrong."

"Spot on," I told him. "Someone tainted Maggie's medication, so it could have been done sometime in the last month for all we know."

Ashton growled a little before he spoke again, and then he stood up from behind his desk. "While it's true that the woman was a thorn in my side, she had a great deal of money invested here. The truth of the matter is that I wouldn't even give her a cross look over an eight-dollar fee, let alone kill her for it." His tune had certainly changed from a few minutes earlier when he hadn't known that Maggie had been murdered.

"But what if she threatened to pull all of that money from your bank?" Grace asked. "That wouldn't look good for you, would it?"

"That's nonsense. People move their assets around for many reasons," Ashton said. "In the end, it all evens out. Besides, she'd been threatening to withdraw her money for years. I never took her seriously."

"Is that *really* why the two of you hated each other so much?" Grace asked him softly.

"I didn't hate her," the banker said, trying his best to keep calm. "She wasn't my favorite customer, but believe it or not, I have some who are worse. A great deal worse, as a matter of fact." He leaned forward and hit a switch on his telephone. "Stella, find out if Maggie Moore is recently deceased."

"How on earth can I do that?" she asked.

"Just call someone in April Springs and ask," he said before slamming the button down again. "Now, if you two will excuse me, I've got a mound of paperwork to catch up on, and then I'm going home to bed and sleep for the next eight hours."

We were ushered out of his office and shown the door rather efficiently, and I had a hunch this wasn't the first time he'd thrown someone out of his office.

Once we were outside, I asked Grace, "Is there any way he killed her over eight dollars?"

"No, if he was telling us the truth," she said.

"About what, exactly?"

"Any of it, Suzanne. We have to confirm that he was at that conference, that he just got back today, and that his only beef with Maggie was over a fee she didn't think she owed. That's three big ifs, if you ask me."

"How do we confirm any of that?" I asked her.

"Simple. Wait right here," she replied as she put on her jacket, did something with her hair, and strolled back into the bank.

I stood there at the Jeep looking silly, so I finally decided just to sit in the driver's seat to wait for her. At least I'd be a little less conspicuous that way. As it was, I felt as though I looked like I was about to be the getaway driver in a bank heist.

Grace came back out less than five minutes later and grinned at me as she walked toward where I was parked.

"What are you smiling about?"

"I spoke with a teller who was quite chatty," Grace said. "Why don't you head back toward April Springs, and I'll tell you all about it."

Once I got us pointed in the right direction, I glanced over at Grace. "Okay, spill it."

"Evidently everything Ashton Belle told us was true. Trudy, that's the teller I spoke with, confirmed that he just got back in town and that she knew it for a fact because she'd been up for hours after driving to Charlotte to pick him up at the airport after his red-eye flight came in from the coast. She was quite grumpy about it and more than willing to vent a little to a sympathetic ear."

"Nice work," I said. Grace was so abrupt occasionally that sometimes I forgot just how charming she could be when she set her mind to it. "What about the animosity between Ashton and Maggie?"

"Evidently Maggie was not averse to making a scene," Grace said. "She came in just before Ashton left for the coast, and the two of them practically had a screaming match in the lobby about that eight-dollar fee he charged her. She was taking it personally, and he wasn't backing down."

I shook my head in wonder. "And you got all of that in less than five minutes? I'm not sure I could have uncovered that much in five days."

"I got lucky picking a chatty teller," Grace said, deflecting a little of my praise. "So, what do we do with the information? I know from what you've told me that Maggie could be pretty abrasive, but even given all of that, it's hard to imagine him killing her over eight dollars."

"I have to agree, unless there's something we don't know about their relationship."

Grace looked horrified by the thought. "Suzanne, do you really think they had a *relationship*?"

"Not that kind of one," I said. "I mean a professional one."

"I guess so," Grace said. "So, we move him down the list, but not entirely off of it. Is that how you want to handle him?"

"It's all we can do at the moment," I said. "I can't believe that one of our first two solid leads has been relegated to the also-ran column."

"Don't be so glum," Grace said. "That still leaves us with Crusty and Jane to go along with Beatrice."

"And not *just* them," I reminded her.

"Do you honestly think that Leanne could have done it?" she asked me.

"At this point I doubt it, though it's still a possibility, but the point I was trying to make was that we can't forget Gabby, either. The two cousins were not on good terms when I saw them together yesterday."

"But what might Gabby's motive be?" Grace asked.

"I'm not sure, but I do think it's something we should check out. Discreetly, of course."

"Of course," Grace answered. "My, we still have quite a bit of work to do today before we're finished, don't we?"

"Yes," I admitted, "but at least the rest of it is going to take place in April Springs. These commutes are killing me."

"I said I would drive," she replied.

"Thanks, but it helps me think when I'm behind the wheel."

"Just save a little of that concentration for the road, if you don't mind," Grace said with a smile.

"I could, but then what fun would that be?" I asked.

"Crusty, would you like some donuts?" I asked as I offered him a box of ten. The man certainly lived up to his name, both in appearance and in disposition. His beard was not white and snowy like Santa's but a bit yellowed and stained instead. Crusty was thin and relatively short, and no one would ever hire him to play jolly old Saint Nick if they saw him. The long-sleeved jacket he was wearing was quite a bit too big for him, and he appeared to be swallowed up in it as he kept trying to free his hands from the folds of clothing.

Crusty looked at my offered box of treats, and then he jacked one eyebrow heavenward. "How much do you want for them? Before you name some outrageous price, I know these are old and stale, so I won't pay more than ten cents on the dollar."

I nearly laughed, but since the man was being dead serious, I knew that I had to respond in kind. "Believe it or not, they aren't even going to cost you that much. They're free, right here and right now, and the offer can expire any second."

He reached out and grabbed the box out of my hands before I could get the final word out. Without a moment's hesitation, he flipped the lid off and looked inside. "There are only ten in here."

"Yes, that's right," Grace said. I could hear a scolding coming on her voice, but we needed information from this man, so I had to cut her off before she could say anything he might take offense to.

"Haven't you heard? Ten is the new twelve," I said lightly. What was that supposed to mean? I didn't know myself, but it seemed to satisfy Crusty.

"Good enough," he said, and then he started to walk away.

"Hang on a second," I called out to him.

"Is there more?" he asked, looking greedily at my empty hands.

"Did you hear about Maggie Moore?" I asked him. There

was no real opportunity to be subtle about it. Crusty wasn't exactly sophisticated when it came to the art of conversation.

"Yep," he said, scratching his beard as though a mouse had infiltrated it and had set up camp. "It's a real shame. Poison is a coward's way to kill."

"Are you saying that it's not your chosen method, then?" Grace asked him archly.

"I'm not about to kill anybody, but if I were to do it, I'd be facing them so that they'd know it was me. I surely didn't kill Maggie, but if I were to do it, it wouldn't have been like that." Crusty frowned for a moment and then shook his head. "I don't want to talk about it. What's done is done. The woman's gone, and no amount of talking is going to bring her back." He seemed a bit cavalier about the whole thing to me, and evidently Grace felt the same way.

"Even though she recently dumped you, you still must feel bad about her passing away," Grace said, trying to feel him out a bit.

"Who told you *she* ended it with *me*?" Crusty asked her, a steel edge coming out in his voice.

"We prefer to keep our sources of information confidential," I told him, "just as we will with whatever you choose to tell us."

"I don't care who you tell," he said with a bit of a cackle in his voice. "For the record, Maggie didn't get rid of me. I thought she was getting a little too serious, so I told her she had to back off. A man needs room to strut, do you know what I mean?"

His reference to strutting matched perfectly with his bantam size and cocky attitude, and I had to smile, though it was only for a split second.

Crusty still managed to catch it, though. "Something I said seem funny to you, Suzanne?" he asked me, staring at me intently.

"No, I know full well that some men aren't meant to be

tamed and tied down," I told him. I wasn't sure how I managed to keep a straight face as I said it, and I only hoped that Grace would be able to do the same.

After a moment of consideration, Crusty seemed to take that at face value. With a brisk nod, he accepted my statement with a slight smile of his own. "What can I say? It pays for a man to keep his options open."

"Like with Jane Preston?" Grace asked him.

That seemed to throw Crusty off his stride. "What are you talking about?"

"We heard that you were wooing her as well," Grace said.

Crusty took that in for a moment before responding. "A gentleman wouldn't comment on something like that."

I felt like telling him that I knew that, and also that the rule didn't exactly apply to him, but I managed to bite my tongue. "Even if you did recently break up with Maggie, that doesn't mean you can't mourn her loss to the world," I said. Though Maggie had been a pain in my neck, albeit briefly, it still didn't mean that she was completely without virtue or that the memory of her should just vanish like a drop of water in a hot skillet.

"What makes you think I'm not?" Crusty asked me. "Not all of us mourn with tears and hysterics," he added.

"When exactly did you two stop going out?" Grace asked him.

"I fail to see how that is any of your business," Crusty said, pulling his box of donuts closer to his chest. "I appreciate the gesture, but if you'll excuse me, I have things to do." No one really knew how Crusty managed to scrape out a living, and I wasn't about to ask him.

"How many women are you seeing at the moment?" Grace asked him.

Crusty didn't even answer. Instead, he turned and walked away from us with his unmistakable walk. I'd seen roosters do the exact same thing, and I had to wonder if Crusty had come by it naturally or if he had painstakingly cultivated it over time.

Once he was gone, Grace looked at me and frowned. "Sorry I drove him off."

"That man was looking for a way to escape the moment he got that box of donuts," I said. "I doubt we would have gotten a straight answer out of him with the use of brute force."

"I guess the real question is, was he hiding his true emotions from us, or did he really not care that Maggie was gone?" Grace asked.

"I'm not sure. He seemed to be a little too casual about the whole thing to me. Maybe Mrs. Preston will be able to shed some light on his true attitude," I said. "If she were dating Crusty as well, something I have an impossible time believing even still, she might be able to help us."

"Then by all means, let's go find her," Grace said. "It's a good thing we've got one final box of donuts left."

"They've been having mixed results, haven't they?" I asked her.

"Well, at the very least they act as an icebreaker. It sure beats walking up to someone and asking them point-blank, 'Did you poison Maggie Moore?'"

"I suppose," I said, "but I know you prefer the direct method of questioning."

Grace laughed. "Suzanne, you've known me my entire life. Has subtlety *ever* been my strong suit?"

"Not that I recall," I agreed.

CHAPTER 12

W̲E̲ ̲W̲E̲R̲E̲ ̲I̲N̲ ̲T̲R̲A̲N̲S̲I̲T̲ ̲T̲O̲ Mrs. Preston's house when Grace's cell phone rang. "Hello? Yes. Of course. Okay. Don't worry about it. We'll do it another time. I understand completely," she finished, and then she put her phone away again.

"I'm guessing the chief cancelled on you again," I said, trying to sound as sympathetic as I could manage to.

"No worries, Suzanne. After our little chat, I was fully expecting it," Grace said, seemingly unfazed by two broken dates in a row. "Besides, I'm still full from lunch, so it works out in my favor anyway."

"We don't have any leftovers to take him tonight, though," I reminded her.

"Do you want to know something? I don't have a problem with that. After all, it won't kill him to fend for himself one night," Grace replied with a grin. "Besides, who are we kidding? If we'd allowed Angelica to give us anything to take with us, we would have already eaten it all by now, regardless of how full we might be."

"You've got a point," I said, happy that Grace was taking Chief Grant's second delay so well. At least I knew she wouldn't sit at home alone tonight pining away for him, not that she would have anyway, but we had an active case ourselves. The fact that it involved the same murder was almost irrelevant.

"Hi, Mrs. Preston," I said when our former teacher answered her door. Even though I hadn't been in her classroom for donkey years, it was a hard habit to break whenever I spoke with her. She had aged over the past year since her husband had died, but she was still a vibrant woman.

"Suzanne. Grace. How lovely to see you both. Please come in."

Mrs. Preston stepped aside and allowed us into her modest bungalow. It had been decorated much as I'd expected, with bright colors and cheerful artwork adorning the walls. Her furniture, though dated, was neat, and nothing in the entire living room appeared to be out of place. Clearly she ran her home as she had kept her classroom, warm and welcoming, but at the same time organized down to the last detail.

A photo of her late husband was displayed prominently over the mantel. "You must miss him terribly," I said. The devotion that couple had felt for each other was legendary in April Springs.

"Every day. Garrison was the love of my life, my true one and only," she said wistfully as she looked at the photo for another moment before turning back to us. "Would you ladies care for some tea? I was just about to have a cup of Earl Grey."

"That would be delightful," I said as I handed her the remaining box of donuts. For some insane reason, I felt the need to apologize for the lack of a true dozen. "I'm sorry to say that there are only ten there," I said, using the same tone of voice I would have used for explaining why my homework wasn't completely finished in time.

"Ten sounds absolutely perfect," she said as she flipped the lid open and peered inside. "Ooh, shall I serve us some right now, or have you had your fill for the day? I can't imagine the temptation you must face each and every day. I know I couldn't do it."

That was hard to believe, especially since she was as tiny as a bird and most likely had the corresponding appetite. "I'll take the tea, but we just had a big lunch," I said, which was strictly true, though a few hours had passed since we'd dined with the DeAngelis clan of women. Grace and I had both eaten so much that I doubted either one of us would be able to even eat any dinner. Well, maybe not a big one, anyway.

"Understood," she said. "I'll be right back. Feel free to make yourselves comfortable."

We did as she suggested, and after Grace and I were sitting beside each other on the couch, I asked her softly, "Can you really see her with Crusty? I think Gabby's lost her mind."

"I'm not about to disagree with that assessment," Grace answered with a grin. "I'm with you. It's inconceivable."

"What is inconceivable?" Mrs. Preston asked as she reentered the living room unexpectedly. "I'm afraid I'm out of Earl Grey. Would something else do?"

"We're fine," I said, not wanting to delay this painful conversation any longer than I had to. "Mrs. Preston, we just spoke with Crusty Lang."

She went absolutely white when I mentioned the man's name. Was it possible that Gabby had somehow been right after all?

"I don't care to discuss that man with you, if you don't mind," she said, killing the conversation completely. At least that was what would have happened if we'd still been in her classroom, but she had lost her position of authority over us, so her word was not necessarily the last one anymore.

"Were you smitten with him?" I asked her, trying to be as sympathetic as I could manage. After all, I knew that opposites sometimes attracted, no matter how hard it might be to believe in this particular case.

"I'd just as soon kiss a snake," she said, her voice filled with silent rage. If Crusty had been the murder victim, my former teacher's name would have instantly gone to the head of my list.

"Why do you hate him so much? Is it because you were competing with Maggie Moore for his attention?" Grace asked her.

The question clearly caught her off guard. "Bite your tongue!" After a momentary pause, she added, "I heard about what happened to Maggie. After all, it's a small town. News travels quickly here."

"How did you two get along, if you weren't romantic rivals?" I asked her.

"Frankly, I didn't care all that much for her. I know it's considered bad manners to speak ill of the dead, but I didn't warm to her the few times we spoke, though I can assure you that it had nothing to do with Crusty."

"Okay, let me get this straight," I said. "You clearly despise Crusty, but it had nothing to do with any romantic situation you two might have been in. If that's the case, I have one question for you. Why do you hate him so much?"

Again, Mrs. Preston's face, in fact her entire body, went rigid. "As I said earlier, I don't care to discuss it. Now, if you two will excuse me, I have important matters to see to."

It was as abrupt a dismissal as I'd ever gotten from her in my life, and I had to admit that it stung a little. "We didn't mean to be insensitive to your situation," I explained, trying to salvage what I could of the situation.

"I'm afraid that I must insist," she said, walking briskly to the door and holding it open for us.

There wasn't much we could do at that point.

So we did as we'd been told and left.

"What was *that* all about?" Grace asked me once we were back in my Jeep.

"Mrs. Preston is clearly upset about something," I said. "Could it possibly be true that she was having a relationship with Crusty Lang, of all people?"

"No, I don't think so," Grace said. "Something else is going on with her, though. She obviously hates Crusty for a reason, but I don't think it has anything to do with romance."

"What could it be, then?" I asked her.

"I'm not sure, but I think we should go back and speak with Crusty again right now," Grace replied.

"Do you honestly think it will do any good?" I asked her.

"No, you're probably right," Grace answered. "Who do we ask, then?"

"I can think of one person who might know," I said.

"I'm game if you are. Who is he?"

"Actually, it's a 'she,'" I said. "We need to ask my mother. If anyone in town knows what's going on with Mrs. Preston, she's the one to speak with."

"Then let's go see what she has to say," Grace said. "Are you going to be okay interrogating your own mother?"

I wasn't, but I was still going to have to somehow find a way to press her. "She and Mrs. Preston have been friends for years. We really don't have much choice."

"Then it's best if we get it over with quickly," Grace said, clearly not any more eager to brace my mother than I was.

"Hey, Momma, do you have a minute?" I asked my mother as she came to the door of the cottage she shared with former police chief Phillip Martin.

"Of course. For you girls, always," she said as she stepped aside and let Grace and me inside. My mother's decorating tastes were similar to Mrs. Preston's, with one distinct difference. I hadn't been able to put my finger on it at the time, but my former schoolteacher's home had a contrived feel to it, as though she were striving to project a certain image over the comfort level of her home. My mother's cottage, on the other hand, felt warm and cozy, a home where love abided. That may have been partly because of my imagination, but I could swear the overall feeling of the place was the difference between a picture of a beam of sunlight and the feeling of the actual warmth on your face.

"Grace, how are you? Looking stylish as always," Momma said before glancing ever so briefly over at me. My mother wasn't a fan of my usual ensembles, but then again, I didn't dress for her. When I wore blue jeans and T-shirts, which was most of the time, I felt the most like myself. On those odd occasions when I had to wear a dress, or even nicer slacks, I counted the minutes until I could get back to my old style again.

I decided to let the subtle dig slip past me. After all, I hadn't come to her for fashion advice, much to her chagrin, I was sure. "We need your help."

"Excellent," Momma said. "If it is in my power, you have it."

I had to grin at my mother. Since I'd moved in with her after my divorce, we'd become close not just as mother and daughter but as two women, even friends. It was an experience that had almost made living through a bad marriage worthwhile.

Almost.

"That's quite a blank check," I said as I hugged her. "Are you sure you don't want to hear what we're asking of you first?"

"I'm sure," she said. "What's going on? Is it your investigation into Maggie Moore's death?"

"How did you know we were digging into that?" I asked, as if I had to even pose the question. I was sure there had to be a dozen ways the word could have gotten back to her. After all, it was no secret that Momma liked to know what her little girl was up to, even if that little girl was now a grown woman.

"Phillip told me," she said, and then she smiled. "He was quite disappointed you didn't call on him to help investigate again."

He'd been a big help to me recently on a case, but Grace was my first choice, with the possible exception of my husband, and everyone knew it. "You don't seem too upset about it."

Momma shrugged, trying to contain her delight. "It has been good experience for the two of you the times you've investigated things together in the past, but I'd hate for it to become a habit. He's most happy when he's digging into transgressions buried far in the past."

I wasn't so sure about that. I'd seen the way he'd thrown himself into the cases we'd worked on together with real gusto, but again, it wasn't my place to point it out to her. "You're still close with Mrs. Preston, aren't you?" I asked, ducking the issue with her husband altogether.

"Jane and I keep in touch. Why do you ask?"

I was about to tell her when Grace did it for me. "Gabby Williams told us that Mrs. Preston was in a battle with Maggie over a man's affections."

"I find that difficult to believe. It couldn't have been much of a contest, could it? What man in his right mind would choose Maggie Moore over Jane Preston?"

"Crusty Lang, at least according to Gabby," I said.

At first, it was clear that Momma thought I was just making another one of my jokes that she never seemed to fully understand, but when she saw me shrug, she reacted instantly. For a petite older woman, she had a fire in her that could match anyone put up against her. "That is the most ridiculous nonsense I've heard in my life. Gabby Williams is either drunk or delusional if she's going around saying such things."

It made me feel better getting Momma's take on it as well, especially since she was so close to my former teacher. "Good. I'm glad to hear that."

When I glanced back at my mother, though, I saw that her smile was quickly fading. "Then again…"

"That's the longest pause I believe I've heard from you, Dot," Grace said, studying my mother carefully. It was clear she was as upset about the prospect that Gabby might have been right as I was.

"You don't think it's actually true, do you?" I asked her, unable to keep the incredulity out of my voice.

"An affair? No, of course not. Her late husband would climb right out of his grave if she even considered it. No, that's not a possibility, but it does explain something I saw the other day at the grocery store."

"What did you see?" I asked her.

"I was chatting with Jane about the atrocious price of oranges when Crusty walked into the store. If I hadn't known better, I would have said that Jane must have seen a ghost. She began to stammer as she ducked behind a cereal display in the aisle, and then she made up a feeble excuse and left me standing there all alone. She had a buggy nearly full of groceries she just abandoned! It was so out of character that I called her later to make sure that she was all right, but she would barely talk to me about it. Clearly *something* is going on there. I just don't know what it is." With that, Momma grabbed her jacket and her purse and started for the door.

"Where are you going?" I asked her as Grace and I filed right behind her.

"Well, it's obvious, isn't it? We're going to go pay Crusty Lang a call."

CHAPTER 13

"**M**OMMA, WE'VE ALREADY SPOKEN WITH him. He wouldn't tell us *anything* about Mrs. Preston."

"Suzanne, I know for a fact that Jane has asked you repeatedly to call her by her first name, and yet you insist on acting as though you were still a child around her."

"That's not true!" I said a little too shrilly. "And besides, Grace does, too."

"I do not!" Grace retorted, sounding remarkably like a kindergartner.

Momma looked at us in turn for just a moment, and then she offered us both smiles as we stood there grinning like a pair of fools. "You two will be the death of me yet."

I hugged her from one side, and Grace from the other. "Maybe so, but not for a very long time, I hope," I said.

"Me, too," Grace added.

Momma, though dwarfed by the two of us, seemed to hover over us as she patted our shoulders simultaneously. "Let's go see what we can uncover."

"We can talk to him all you want, but I've got a hunch that he's not going to tell you any more than he did us," I warned her.

"Ah, but that's where you're wrong," Momma said. She hesitated once we were outside, studying my Jeep and then looking at her much nicer, and larger, vehicle. "Shall I drive?"

"Come on, be a sport. Let's take mine," I said with a smile. "You can even ride up in front. Right, Grace?" I asked, biting my lower lip as I looked at her. I'd offered her normal seat to my mother without consulting her, but I was certain that she would not only understand but heartily approve as well.

"Are you kidding me? I *love* riding around in back being chauffeured around town," Grace said. "It makes me feel important."

"I'm certain you don't need a driver to feel that way," Momma said, but she still climbed into the passenger seat beside me.

As I drove us all to Crusty's place, I asked Momma, "So, would you mind telling us why Crusty will talk to you but not us?"

"Suzanne, I know more about that man than he realizes. I can apply pressure to the correct points to make him come clean with us within seven minutes. What's more, I guarantee it."

"Wow, what kind of dirt do you have on him, Dot?" Grace asked from her position behind us.

"I don't feel comfortable sharing that with the two of you," Momma answered a little primly.

"Come on, we'll be right there when you use the thumbscrews on him, so we'll hear all about it then," I reminded her.

"We shall see," was all that I could get Momma to say. I did my best to drive a little slower and a bit more carefully than normal, but that still didn't stop her from clutching her seat belt like a lifeline and applying imaginary brakes every twelve feet of the journey. It was like having her teach me to drive all over again, an experience that neither one of us had relished. Still, it had been part of the ritual that was my upbringing, and as angry as I'd been with her at the time, at least I could look back on it fondly now.

Crusty was out front, trimming a large overgrown plant that was threatening to take over his yard, when we got there. I'd noticed the bush on our earlier visit, but I hadn't really given it much thought. He was sweating profusely from his efforts, but he still quickly threw on that same oversized jacket we'd seen earlier the moment he realized we were there. There were a few welts on his arms, and I had to wonder if he'd gotten a little too close to the shrub he'd just been trimming and if it had reached out and grabbed him.

"Why are you back, Suzanne?" he asked me with a less than welcoming tone of voice.

And then he saw my mother get out of the passenger seat of my Jeep.

"Dot? What are you doing here? I wasn't expecting you," he said as he tried in vain to straighten his collar.

"We need to have ourselves a little chat, Crusty," Momma said brightly, but I could also hear the edge of steel in her words, and I was positive that Crusty hadn't missed it, either.

"There's really no need. I told the girls all I know before," he said as he frowned, staring at the length of branch in his hand he had been ready to sever.

She pointed toward a small garden patch he kept. "You need to keep those runners pruned, or you'll be overrun with pumpkins next month," Momma told him. Was it possible she was making a point about something *other* than pumpkins? "It's a shame when things don't cooperate, isn't it? Don't you just hate it when you have to take matters into your own hands and intervene?"

I knew that she wasn't still talking about the vines anymore now, and I caught a glimpse of Crusty's expression to make sure that he had gotten the message as well.

His face was as white as Mrs. Preston's had been earlier.

What exactly did my mother have on this man, anyway?

It was clear from his stance that he was considering fighting back and refusing to accept my mother's not-so-subtle hints, but then he must have looked into her eyes, and I could see him crumple right in front of us. I knew my mother could back down a mountain lion, but the control she wielded over this man was nothing short of amazing. "Can I have a word with you in private, ma'am? Please?" he added. I wasn't a big fan of the man, but his broken spirit still touched me.

I wasn't going to let him have a private audience with my mother though, no matter how bad I felt for him. After all, a killer was loose in April Springs, and I wasn't going to let my mother be the next victim if I had anything to say about it. "That's not a great idea, Momma," I told her.

"Listen to Suzanne, Dot," Grace said beside me.

"Girls, I appreciate your concern, but there's no need to be alarmed. Crusty and I are just going to have a nice little chat over in the shade, aren't we, Crusty?"

He couldn't even meet her gaze now. "Yes, ma'am."

If I hadn't seen it with my own eyes, I wouldn't have believed it. My respect for my mother, already at a pretty high level, was growing by leaps and bounds.

"We'll be right over there," I said as I pointed to the Jeep. "If you need us, just raise your voice, and we'll come running."

"You know I rarely raise my voice," Momma said as she patted my hand. "Don't worry. It will be fine."

"Sure. Of course it will," I said as Grace and I headed the fifty feet back to my Jeep. "If he makes one move toward Momma with those clippers, I'm going for his throat."

Grace nodded. "I think he knows that," she said as she pointed back at the two of them. Crusty had dropped the clippers completely, and somehow, even given his bantam status, he seemed to shrink within himself even further.

After three minutes, with a few scornful glares and admonitions from my mother, she came back to the Jeep. I hated it when she turned her back on the man, but he was clearly beaten down, and I didn't think he had an ounce of fire left in him.

"What did he tell you?" I asked her.

"We need to pay Jane a visit now," Momma said, ignoring my question. I had learned that move from the master, but that didn't mean I was willing to accept it.

"Come on. You've *got* to tell us." I realized I was sounding a bit like an entitled little brat even as I said it, but I couldn't seem to help myself.

"This is not related to Maggie Moore's murder," she said.

"And we're just supposed to take your word for it?" I asked her.

"That would be nice, of course," she answered serenely. I'd thought about refusing to drive to Mrs. Preston's until we got more information, but in the end, I didn't have any more spirit than Crusty had.

I caved in.

"Can you at least give us a hint about what he said to you?" Grace asked meekly from the back seat. My mother was the only one who could do that to her, but then again, it wasn't all that surprising to me.

"No, dear." Her plain denial was more effective than the most effusive argument, because if she refused to engage with us, there was no way we were going to get her to talk.

I reached for the radio dial when Momma asked kindly, "If you don't mind, could we just ride in silence? I have to be very careful how I handle this."

"If you'd like some advice, Grace and I are eager and willing to supply it," I said with an exaggerated grin.

"As much as I appreciate the offer, I'm fine," she replied.

When we got to Mrs. Preston's place, Momma asked us, "Would

you two mind waiting here? Better yet, I can get Phillip to come get me when I'm finished."

"Sorry, but that's not happening," I told her firmly. "As much as I love Mrs. Preston, she's still a suspect in an active investigation, no matter how much you vouch for her. I can't stop you from going in alone, but I can surely stand watch out here, so make sure she knows that, will you?"

Momma reached out and patted my hand. "Suzanne, you truly are concerned for my safety, aren't you?"

"I am, too," Grace said from the back. "I want to go on the record saying that this is a very bad idea, Dot."

"Exception noted, dear," Momma said. "Still, it is something I must do."

"Then do me one favor, would you?" Grace asked her.

"What is that?"

"If she offers you anything to eat or drink, please say no, no matter how rude it might sound to you. Will you do that, for me?"

"For us," I said, happy that Grace had thought of it. After all, we were dealing with a potential poisoner. How foolish would it be to take *anything* from her that might be tainted? Thank goodness she'd been out of Earl Grey tea earlier. Grace and I were going to have to start taking our own advice to refuse food and drink from any of our suspects, or one of us might end up on the dead list next.

"I will be careful. I promise you both."

Momma squeezed our hands, even reaching across the backrest toward Grace, and then she mounted the steps with confidence and aplomb. I loved her—I kind of had to since she was my mother—but I admired her as well, and that didn't come so freely given.

"Hey there," I said loudly when Mrs. Preston came out to answer the door. I wanted to make sure beyond a shadow of a doubt that she knew we were there, and now Momma didn't have to tell her.

Once they were inside, I turned back to look at Grace. "Are we doing the right thing here?"

"What choice did we have?" she asked me. "I'm not about to tell your mother she can't do something. Are you?"

"You don't even have to ask," I said. "I'm still worried sick about her."

"We'll give her ten minutes, and no matter what she says, there's going to be a 'family emergency' that she has to see to immediately. Agreed?" Grace asked me.

We shook on it.

Nine minutes later, I had my hand on the car door.

"Where do you think you're going?" Grace asked me. "We have to give her another full minute. That was our arrangement."

"I can give her the time walking to the door, can't I?" I asked.

I didn't need to even do that much, though.

Before I could get out of the Jeep, Momma left the house and joined us.

I was so relieved I couldn't speak, but then I saw the tears tracking down her cheeks.

What exactly had just happened in there?

CHAPTER 14

"**I** DON'T WANT TO TALK ABOUT what just happened in there, so don't ask me," Momma said as she got in, dabbing at her cheeks as she tried to dry her tears. When I didn't make a move to start the Jeep, she looked at me oddly. "Don't tell me it won't start, Suzanne."

"It won't until I turn the key," I said as I sat there resolutely.

"Young lady," she said in that scolding tone that had withered me in the past.

"Sorry. I can't help you." It took all that I had to refuse her, but this was getting ridiculous. We couldn't eliminate suspects based on only my mother's word, no matter how much I trusted it. If I was going to run my investigations that way, I might as well not even bother.

"Grace, will you please talk some sense into her?" Momma asked as she turned to the back seat.

"I'm sorry," Grace said. It was one thing to always claim that she had my back, but standing up to my mother proved it beyond any words. "I agree with Suzanne. We *have* to know. Dot, you should know that you can trust us to be discreet, but we truly do have to know."

Momma sat there for a few moments stewing about our open rebellion, and I was happy this wasn't July or August. At least we didn't need air conditioning. As a matter of fact, if anything, it felt a bit frosty in the Jeep at the moment.

Momma finally let out a sigh and nodded. "You're right. I

somehow seem to think of you two as the little girls who had sleepovers in your treehouse a very long time ago, but you're both grown women now. Crusty was blackmailing Jane, or at least he was trying to. It had nothing to do with what happened to Maggie, and it certainly wasn't any rivalry over Crusty's affections."

Wow. I always thought of blackmailers as wicked strangers who hid in the shadows, not a cocky little rooster of a man who considered himself a gift to women everywhere. "Was he trying to get her to sleep with him?" I asked. I wasn't sure Mrs. Preston would have anything worth protecting to make her give in to that particular demand, but I could honestly see Crusty trying.

"Suzanne, don't be tawdry," Momma scolded me.

"As though blackmail isn't crude enough in and of itself," I countered.

"That's a fair point," she conceded.

"What was he blackmailing her for then?" Grace asked. "She can't have all that much money."

"You'd be surprised. Her husband had a substantial insurance policy, and Jane has never been all that extravagant in her spending. She's managed to save quite a tidy sum over the years."

"I still don't understand why she would be in a position to be blackmailed in the first place," I said. I knew that Grace had to have been thinking the same thing as well, but we could have stayed there all day and she wouldn't have brought it up. She was willing to push my mother's boundaries somewhat, but not nearly as far as I was willing to.

"That I will not tell you," Momma said. "Jane gave me a little latitude in what I could and could not disclose to the two of you, but she insists that she take the reason to her grave. She told me in confidence, and I won't violate it. Needless to say, it's something she would fight with her last breath to protect."

"Is there any chance that *Maggie* knew about it?" I asked, getting a sudden burst of insight.

Momma looked shocked by the suggestion. "I don't see how."

"Crusty found out, and if he was trying to win Maggie back, maybe he told her about Mrs. Preston, trying to impress her. It's possible, isn't it?"

"Yes," Momma said, sagging low in her seat. "I don't want to admit it, but I can see that as a possibility."

"So then Jane and Crusty still need to be prime suspects in Maggie Moore's murder," I said.

"You called her Jane for the first time in your life," Momma replied. "Did you even realize that you did that?"

"Well, maybe it's because this is the first time I'm seeing her as something other than my former schoolteacher," I answered.

"Suzanne, I still can't even bring myself to consider the possibility that she killed Maggie," Momma said.

"That couldn't be wishful thinking, could it?" I asked.

"Yes, I suppose it could," Momma replied.

"Then they both stay on our list." I started the Jeep and headed back to Momma's place.

"Where are we going now?" she asked me.

"I'm taking you home," I said.

"I still have some time before I need to get back home," Momma said. "I could always go with you."

"Thanks, but we'll call you if we need you again," I said with a smile.

"Is it because I balked initially on sharing anything with you?" Momma asked in a soft voice as we pulled up in front of her cottage. She sounded contrite as she spoke, something I wasn't used to hearing from her.

I turned off the ignition, unbuckled my seat belt, and leaned in to hug her. "No, ma'am. You did the right thing, and I respect you for it. Your friends are important to you."

"True, but no one is more important to me than my family,"

she answered, and then she turned to Grace. "I hope you know that includes you as well."

"I appreciate that more than I can say," Grace answered.

"Very well then," Momma said as she opened her door. "Keep me posted with your progress. At least promise me that much."

"We'll do that," I said.

Once Momma was gone, Grace moved up to her usual seat. "May I ask you something, Suzanne?"

I thought surely that it was going to be about what we'd just learned, or perhaps even the fact that Momma had just told her that she was one of us. "Of course."

"Are you as hungry as I am?" she asked me seriously.

I burst out laughing. "*That's* your question?"

"Sure, what else would be so important?" she asked me.

"Never mind. Sure, I could eat," I said. Though we'd recently lunched like royalty, it seemed like a lifetime ago. "How does the Boxcar sound?"

"Like a dream come true," Grace said with a grin.

Just as I pulled up into the parking lot, Grace's cell phone rang. After glancing at the caller ID, she said, "That's my boss. I'd better get that."

"She *does* know that you're working half days this week, right?" I asked her.

"Technically speaking?"

"Grace?" I asked her, scolding a little with my tone.

"Shush," she said as she got out of the Jeep before she answered it.

I got out, too, and while I was waiting for her to finish her call, I saw Leanne coming out of the grill. "Hey there," I said.

She had been so distracted by something that she hadn't even noticed me until I'd spoken to her. "Suzanne. What are you doing here?"

"I thought I might get a bite to eat," I told her.

"Of course. I'm sorry. I'm just not myself right now. This whole thing with Maggie has got me flustered more than I can say."

I studied Leanne and saw that she was indeed a little off her game. As she tugged at her long-sleeved shirt, I saw that she had a rather substantial bandage on one hand. "What happened to you there?"

She looked down at the injury and shrugged. "That stupid oven Maggie bought has a sharp edge that catches me every time I take something out of the oven. I was going to have her hire someone to do something about it before we opened, but I'm not entirely sure I can do this on my own now. I needed my aunt a great deal, and what's worse, I miss her. I know she could be prickly at times, but if you dug down deep enough, she really was sweet."

I wondered just how deep you'd have to dig, but I didn't say anything to her. "Have you made any decisions yet about your future?"

"No. All I know for sure is that I would never have dreamed of opening a shop like we were going to have without her at the helm running things."

"I know you told me before, but you honestly didn't want to be a partner in the business?" I asked her.

Leanne's expression was clear and immediate. "No thank you. Not a chance. Who needs the headaches? The *only* thing I've ever wanted to do in my life is make pies. As a baker yourself, I'm sure you understand why I feel that way, Suzanne."

I should have nodded in agreement, but instead, I decided it was the perfect time to probe a little while Gabby wasn't around.

"Leanne, I've been dancing around something since yesterday, but we need to talk about it if you're up to it."

The young woman bit her lower lip for a moment, and I wondered if she was about to cry, but if so, she managed to rein it in. "Go on."

"Did you know about Maggie publishing a cookbook?"

"Of course I did," Leanne said, studying me with a curious expression. "Why have you been worried about bringing *that* up?"

"I just can't imagine how angry you must have been when you found out that she stole your pie cookbook from you and published it herself. You must have been furious when you found out."

"What do you mean, found out? I *gave* Maggie those recipes! I didn't want *any* credit, it was just to help the shop, but she promised to split the earnings right down the middle with me anyway, and to be honest with you, that was fine with me, since I would never have done it on my own. *I* came to *her* with the idea, Suzanne. I wanted those recipes out in the world, but if it hadn't been for Maggie, it never would have happened. I'm delighted that we were able to do one last project together. Besides, she was nearly broke. Opening the pie shop took nearly everything she had. She's been watching pennies for years in order to do it, and she'd sunk just about every dime she'd saved into it. Why shouldn't she share in the royalties generated by our recipes?"

Leanne clearly meant what she was saying. Wow, I had clearly read the situation all wrong, as did Gabby. Then again, why did that surprise me? Gabby had gotten quite a bit wrong lately. She was definitely slipping. "So, what are you going to do about the pie shop?"

"I don't know," she said, clearly sounding exasperated. "I

may just try to make a go of it after all. I've had several people graciously offer to help."

"Well, if you ask me, this town could *always* use a pie shop," I answered with a grin. "Since the bakery went out of business, we've needed something more than store-bought desserts."

"Doesn't that include you and your donut shop?" she asked me.

"No, try as I might, I haven't been able to persuade people around here to finish their meals with a donut or two for dessert."

"How's your investigation going? The police won't tell me anything," Leanne said.

"We're making real progress," I said. "I think we'll be able to solve it sooner rather than later." It was sheer bluff on my part, but I had to give the woman something to hang her hopes on.

Leanne was about to reply when her cell phone rang. "It's Aunt Gabby," she said. "I swear, I know the woman cares for me, but does that mean she has to know where I am around the clock? She won't even let me go to the pie shop without an escort, and it's driving me a little crazy."

"I'm sure that she can be smothering at times, but at least it's better to be loved too much than not at all," I said.

"I suppose so," she said with the hint of a grin. "Sorry. I hate to be rude, but if I don't take this, the police chief will be out looking for me in two minutes."

As Leanne walked away and took the call, Grace rejoined me.

"How did your call with your boss go?"

"It was nothing," Grace answered. "She just needed a contact number for one of my people." She gestured to Leanne's retreating form. "What was that all about?"

"Well, Leanne claims that having her aunt write the pie-making cookbook was her idea and that she was grateful that Maggie stepped in and made it a reality."

"Did you believe her?" Grace asked me.

"Do you want to know what? I think I do," I answered.

"But you're not one hundred percent sure," she pushed.

"No, but maybe ninety, ninety-five percent."

"Okay, we'll keep that in mind. What about her other motive?"

"The pie shop? Leanne insisted that she wanted no part of being a co-owner of the shop, that all she wanted to do was bake. I can certainly understand that feeling. She's had some folks in town offer to help her out, but she hasn't made up her mind yet. Personally, I think she's going to do it. After all, what else does she have at this point?"

"I don't know if I could move forward if I were in her shoes," Grace said.

"Why not?"

"Could you work in a place every day where your aunt was murdered, Suzanne? I'm sure that I'd see the woman's ghost around every corner."

"Yes, I see what you mean," I said. My stomach rumbled a bit, more from the promise of food than actual hunger, I was sure. "Let's go grab something to eat so we can get back to work."

"I like your priorities," Grace said with a smile as we climbed the steps of the Boxcar Grill and went inside.

"I was just about to call you," Trish said furtively as Grace and I walked in. Without another word, she pulled me back into the kitchen, with Grace following close behind. Gladys, the only cook on duty currently, smiled at me briefly, and I returned the favor. She'd been instrumental in saving both Grace and me once upon a time when we'd confronted a killer, and the older woman would always have a soft spot in my heart for her heroic actions.

"What's so urgent?" I asked Trish.

"Do you two know a woman named Beatrice Branch?" she asked me.

"Yes, she was Maggie Moore's sister-in-law once. Why do you ask?"

"She came into the diner ten minutes ago trying to pry any information she could out of me about both of you, that's why," Trish said, tugging at her ponytail, a sure sign she was worried.

"Well, I suppose that's only fair, since we've been asking folks about her since I saw Maggie's body lying in the pie shop," I answered.

I must have been a little calmer about the whole thing than Trish liked. "So, let me get this straight. She's a suspect in Maggie's murder, and you're treating her interest in you lightly? Is that smart?"

"What makes you think she's a suspect?" I asked, ducking the question for the moment.

"Come on, if she was related to Maggie, she's bound to be, isn't she? What's her story, anyway?"

I looked at Grace, who simply shrugged. It was obvious she didn't care if I told Trish about what we'd uncovered or not, so I didn't have to think much about bringing her up to speed. "Beatrice believes that Maggie poisoned her brother, though no one could ever prove it at the time of his death. Besides that, she had a pretty large financial interest in Maggie not living another three days." Wow, it really did sound bad when I said it like that.

"And you're not worried?" she asked me. "Grace, talk some sense into her, would you?"

"If anything, I think it's a good sign," Grace said. "We're rattling some cages, so of course there are folks who are going to resent it. Is she still here, by any chance?"

Trish nodded. "I don't understand either one of you, but as long as you both seem to get each other, I suppose I'll have to accept it. She's still sitting at a table in the back, trying to pin down Thad Belmont about the two of you."

I knew Thad well from the donut shop. Beatrice had chosen the wrong man to seek information from. Thad was the biggest gossip in April Springs, but the trouble was you could only believe a fourth of the information you heard from him. What was more, he'd been known to practice a little friendly extortion while hanging tantalizing bits in the air that usually led nowhere. I had a feeling that he was going to ride that horse as long as he could, and then he was going to pull the rug out from under her. "What has he gotten out of her so far? I hope she's at least buying him dessert."

"Actually, she paid for his entire meal," Trish said with a grin. Even though she was worried about Grace and me, she couldn't help but display some amusement at Thad's behavior.

"Should we give him more time to get that dessert before we go out?" I asked Grace.

"No, he should be happy with what he's managed to squeeze out from her so far," she said.

I stopped to pat Trish's shoulder. "Thanks for worrying about us."

"Why wouldn't I? You two are my best friends," she said, and then she added with a grin, "Sad, isn't it?"

"More than I can tell you," I said as I hugged her, with Grace quickly following suit.

Trish followed us into the dining room, as I knew she would. Grace and I walked back to the table where Thad was holding court, talking about the two of us to one of our prime suspects. None of what he was saying was even remotely true, and he winked at me when he realized that he'd been caught in the act.

I had to give him credit for that. He might not have had truth on his side, but he certainly had confidence in his presentation.

"Ladies, we were just talking about you," Thad said as he stood. "I believe you know my dinner companion."

At least Beatrice had the good grace to look embarrassed at getting caught. She had on another long-sleeved blouse, but this one didn't manage to cover her arms as well as the last one had. Was that a bandage sticking out from one of the cuffs? I couldn't be sure, because the moment she noticed me looking, she tugged at it self-consciously. "I've been looking all over town for you two," she said as brightly as she could, though I noticed that she couldn't make eye contact with either one of us as she said it.

"Well, what do you know? We were right here all along," I said as I took a seat at their table.

Beatrice didn't look too pleased by that development, and when Grace braced her on the other side, she actually started squirming a little in her seat. Beatrice somehow managed to knock her purse over in the process, and I spied something that looked like a photocopied blueprint inside it before she hurriedly bundled it all back together. Thad was in paradise as he settled back into his own chair to watch the show. The only problem with that was I didn't particularly want an audience. "Thad, is Trish motioning for you to join her?"

He didn't even look in her direction as he pushed his empty dinner plate aside. "That's okay. I'll catch up with her later."

Trish saw that she was being ignored, and then she had a stroke of brilliance. Ducking back into the kitchen for a moment, she emerged again with a piece of orange pineapple cake. I knew from personal experience that the cake was just about the best thing I'd ever tasted in my life, and that was really saying something.

"You might want to look," I said sternly.

He appeared not to want to be bothered, but when he saw

Trish offering him a substantial slice of cake, he was out of his seat in no time. I had a hunch that the only thing more alluring to the man than gossip was dessert. "I'll be right back," he said as he stood.

"Take your time," I answered, getting his attention and warning him with a single glance that he didn't want to poke this particular bear just now.

He got the message. "I will, then. Ladies," he said, tipping a hat that wasn't there, and then he hurried off before Trish had the chance to change her mind.

"That man treated me like a fool," Beatrice said huffily once he was gone.

"What happened? Did he not deliver when you tried to bribe him with a free meal?" Grace asked her sweetly, though there was no warmth in her voice as she did so.

"I don't know what you're talking about," Beatrice said after pausing too long before coming up with a believable response.

"Of course you don't," Grace said.

"Why were you looking for us?" I asked her before she had a chance to rebound from Grace's sarcasm.

"I have information for you," Beatrice said firmly.

"About?" I asked, though I knew full well what she was talking about.

"Maggie Moore's death," Beatrice said sharply.

"Murder, you mean," Grace corrected her harshly.

"Yes, of course," Beatrice replied. "Murder."

"Why come to us? Shouldn't you go straight to the police if you know something?" I asked her.

"They don't want to listen to what I have to say, but perhaps you will," Beatrice said.

"We'll certainly hear you out, and you don't even have to buy our meals," Grace said happily.

Beatrice chose to ignore her comment. Instead, she focused

on me. "So tell me, Suzanne, do you want to know what I have to say, or not?"

"I want to know," I said. Enough with this cat and mouse.

"Correction," Grace added. "*We* want to know."

"Very well," she answered. "I have information that might just crack this case wide open."

CHAPTER 15

"**G**O ON. WE'RE LISTENING," I told her as I glanced over at Grace. She looked just as confused as I was. What exactly was going on here?

"Did you know that Crusty stole money from Maggie just before she died?" she asked with a knowing look on her face. "That's why he probably killed her, so she wouldn't go to the police about it and have him arrested."

We hadn't heard anything about this wild theory, and given what we'd learned from other sources, it didn't make much sense. We knew that Maggie had sunk most of her money into the pie shop, so what was there for Crusty to steal? Leanne had told us that Maggie had put just about every dime she'd made in the past few years into establishing it. "That doesn't jibe with what we've heard from other sources," I said.

I was about to allow that it was possible, but before I could say another word, Beatrice shrugged off my objection with something brand new. "Okay then, if you don't like that, how about this? Gabby had her own reasons to kill her cousin," Beatrice said with a frown. "Have you even considered her? Of course not, she's a friend of yours, and you don't think she's capable of a crime like murder."

"We have our doubts that she did it, but it has nothing to do with our friendship with her," Grace said. It was odd hearing my best friend defend the woman, given their rocky relationship, but it was true enough. "It doesn't fit her character, plus Gabby is working with us earnestly to help solve the crime. Doesn't that tell you that she's innocent?"

Beatrice shrugged. "I'm working with you, too! What do you call this?" She paused a moment, and then she asked, "What if she's helping just to keep you from discovering the truth?"

It was a possibility, and one I hadn't really considered as of yet. Was Gabby really that diabolical? I didn't think so, but I'd been wrong before. Then again, if that rationale applied to Gabby, then it had to apply to Beatrice as well, given her own statement a moment ago. "Okay, let's suppose for a second that Gabby killed Maggie. What motive would she have?"

"Come on, that's easy. You know how abrasive Maggie was," Beatrice snapped. "Everyone who ever knew her had a motive to poison those pills."

"Maybe so, but Gabby cares for her family above all else, even the people she doesn't particularly like. Her emotions run deep, and without another motive better than irritation, I'm not sure she deserves to even be mentioned in the same breath as our other suspects." You included, I wanted to add, but I wanted to see what else Beatrice would claim to know. With any luck, she might just end up hanging herself.

One could only hope.

"Fine. Maybe Gabby didn't do it. Surely you have to consider Jane Preston, though. She had reason enough to hate Maggie. After all, they were rivals for Crusty's affections, and you know how that can infect people's emotions and actions. She was getting rid of a rival."

"I don't know who your source of information is, but we disproved that theory today. Jane's beef was with Crusty, not with Maggie. Beatrice, what's this really all about? Are you possibly trying to distract us from the fact that *you* had the most motive of all to see the woman dead?"

"That's ridiculous," Beatrice said a little more strongly than she probably should have. "What about her business partner, Leanne? It's a joke calling her that; she was nothing more than an employee."

"True, but only because that's the way Leanne wanted it," Grace told her. "Is that the best you can do?"

"How about the pie recipe book?" she asked triumphantly. "Did you even know about that? There was going to be loads of money made off of that, and Maggie stole every last recipe from Leanne."

"Again, you're way off base, Beatrice," I told her. "Leanne was happy with both arrangements. Now stop grasping at straws and tell us the truth. Why are you trying to sully everyone else's name but your own? Is it to keep us off your trail?"

"*Trail?*" she asked angrily. "There's no trail, because I didn't kill the woman, and I won't sit here and listen to this nonsense anymore."

"Why not?" Grace asked her. "That's exactly what you just asked us to do. All you *did* was spout nonsense."

"You'll see," Beatrice said, shaking a finger at both of us angrily as her face continued to redden. "When the truth comes out, you'll both be sorry."

And then she stormed out, the perfect exit.

Trish came over to join us after Beatrice left the diner. "What was that all about? I was carrying a tub of dirty dishes, and that woman nearly knocked it out of my hands in her rush to get out of here so quickly."

"I couldn't say. We were just having a little chat," I said as innocently as I could manage.

Trish clearly didn't believe me, but then again, she also must have noticed that half a dozen of her patrons were paying particularly close attention to us. "Okay. Whatever you say." In a softer voice, she added as she leaned forward, "You two had better hope that she's not the murderer. By the look on her face as she left here, she's ready to kill you both."

"Sometimes we have to stir the pot to get results," Grace said.

"And there are times when the pot boils over anyway, despite your best efforts to contain it. Just be sure that what happened to Maggie doesn't happen to the two of you. Believe it or not, I've grown awfully fond of you both over the years, so I'd hate to see anything happen to either one of you."

"We would, too," I said with a smile. "Now that Beatrice is gone, what are the chances we can get two of your specials for dinner?" I glanced at Grace and added, "I don't mean to order for you. You can have whatever you'd like."

"Really? Anything? Gosh, you're the best friend a girl could ever have."

We both busted out laughing, and Trish soon joined us.

The rest of the diner looked at us all as though we were crazy.

In truth, maybe we were. We'd gone out of our way to antagonize one of our primary suspects in Maggie Moore's murder, and Trish wasn't completely out of bounds when she'd suggested that it might not have been a good idea to purposely anger a possible killer. Then again, we couldn't just sit back and wait for things to happen. Grace and I believed that sooner was almost always better than later, and if it took a little pressure—and risk as well—it was probably worth it.

The meal was amazing; Gladys had outdone herself. She'd once been temporary, filling in only when needed, but her skills had elevated enough to go to work on a full-time basis, though she usually just cooked either late at night or very early in the morning. The country-style steak had been done to perfection, the homemade mashed potatoes were smooth and creamy, and the skillet-fried green beans had the perfect amount of seasoning and crispness to them. Had she been taking cooking lessons? Or more likely, had someone else given her a hand in the kitchen before we'd arrived? My money was on the latter instead of the former. After we finished eating, we lingered a bit at the table, sipping our sweet tea, neither one of us ready to go back out into the world and grill another suspect.

Grace asked, "What do you think about Beatrice's little performance earlier?"

"It did feel a bit staged, didn't it?" I asked her.

"The first part of it, anyway. There at the end, it was almost as though she was coming up with theories on the fly. I half expected her to blame us for Maggie's murder before she left."

"It wouldn't have surprised me."

"She did get me to thinking, though," Grace said after a few moments of silence.

"Well, stranger things have happened," I said with a grin. "What did she trigger?"

"Is it possible that Crusty really *did* steal money from Maggie?"

"I know Leanne said she sank every penny she had into the pie shop, but what if there was more going on behind closed doors than she knew? Maggie didn't exactly seem the type to share everything with her employee, did she?"

"I wouldn't think so," Grace said with a frown.

"What are you so troubled by?" I asked her.

"I was just hoping that we wouldn't have to go back to Crusty's yet again," she said.

"We have to, though, don't we?"

"I don't see any way around it, and the sooner the better, too," Grace said as she stood.

"Let's split the bill tonight," I said. My friend had been picking up far too many tabs lately, and I didn't want it to get to be a habit for either one of us.

"I wasn't going to suggest we do anything else," she said with a shrug.

I didn't believe her for one second, but I did appreciate her trying to allow me to at least try to save a little face.

Unfortunately, Crusty wasn't home when we got there. There was a pile of freshly trimmed branches at the curb, and I knew that the town workers would be picking them up in the morning. I had knocked on the door, rung the bell, and knocked again, even though his vehicle was gone, all to no avail.

"What do you think we should do now?" Grace asked as she frowned, looking around for someone to blame for the man's absence.

"Short of camping out on his doorstep, I don't think we have much choice, and we both know that I'm not that far from my bedtime. Thank goodness Emma and Sharon are coming back in a few days. I got a text message from my assistant while we were eating. It's been nice not having to pay her wages, but the work is killing me."

"I get that," Grace said as she headed back toward the Jeep.

I walked with her, but I stopped after a few steps, though.

I was poking around in the bush Crusty had been cutting earlier when Grace rejoined me. "Suzanne, what are you doing?"

I ran my hands across the leaves and branches, and I was surprised to find that they yielded easily to my touch, thin and pliable, but more importantly, not a single thorn on any stem I touched. "This branch is harmless."

"So?"

"Crusty was a little late putting his jacket on the last time we were here," I said. "I happened to notice that there were welts, almost like scratches, all over his arms before he could cover them up."

"But this bush doesn't have anything that might cause that," Grace said as she ran her hands over some of the nearby branches as well.

"No, but the ones at the pie shop certainly did," I said.

"Do we think Crusty did it now?" Grace asked me.

"Well, the truth of the matter is that he wasn't the only one a little scratched up," I said. "Not only was Beatrice wearing long-sleeved blouses every time we've seen her, but I saw the hint of a bandage on one of her arms. It could have easily been covering up a scratch. Also, Leanne had a bandage on her arm as well, but I know I've certainly scratched myself enough working in a tight kitchen, so at least she has a plausible excuse."

"Suzanne, is it possible that we are both being so paranoid that we are seeing clues that aren't really there?"

"Anything is possible at this point," I said. "There's no use hanging around here. We have no idea when, or even if, Crusty is coming back."

Just as I said it, though, the man in question drove up and parked in his driveway beside my Jeep, and he was clearly as unhappy as we were seeing him yet again.

"What do you two want?" he asked us, no sign of civility at all in his voice. "I thought things were finally settled between us."

"How did you hurt your arm, Crusty?" I asked him, abiding by his wishes to get to the point without fanfare.

"This?" he asked. "If I said it was none of your business, would you leave me alone?"

"No," I said, "but if you tell us the truth about two things, we'll go away."

"For tonight," Grace amended.

It was a good save. After all, I didn't want to make any promises I had no intention of keeping.

"I scratched it on some bushes I was trimming," he said with a frown.

"But these aren't scratchy," I said as I ran my hand over the bush in question again.

"True, but they aren't the only ones I cut over the past few days. The ones in back are kind of prickly, just like the two of you."

The slam didn't bother me, nor did it register with Grace, based on her lack of recognition. "Could we see them?" she asked him.

"You may not," he said. "What's the second question?"

"Did you steal money from Maggie Moore just before she died?" I asked him.

He laughed long and hard at the accusation, a reaction I hadn't been expecting. "Maggie sank nearly every dime she had into that stupid pie shop of hers. There was nothing to steal."

So, Leanne's story about Maggie's financial situation checked out, and Beatrice's suggestion turned out to be exactly what it had seemed at the time, a woman desperate to divert attention from herself.

"I'd still like to see those bushes," I said.

"And I'd like a million dollars, but I don't think either one of us is going to be happy tonight. Now I'll ask you both to kindly leave my property." Crusty took a few steps toward the door before stopping suddenly and turning around. "One more thing. If I catch either one of you lurking around in my backyard, you'll regret it. I promise you that."

"Is that a threat, Crusty?" I asked him pointedly. I hated being bullied, and I knew that the only way to beat one was to stand up to him. Unless of course he turned out to be a psychopathic mad-dog killer, and in that case, I'd just poked a monster that should have been left alone.

"It's a promise," he said. With a grin that had no warmth in it, he added softly, "My eyesight isn't what it once was. If I saw someone prowling around my backyard, I might think it was a burglar, and if that were the case, you should know that I'm never very far away from my gun."

Once he was back inside, Grace studied me a moment. "I don't know about you, but I'm willing to risk it if you are. I think he's bluffing."

"But what if he's not?" I asked her.

"I suppose you pay your money and you take your chances," Grace said, though without much enthusiasm.

I didn't blame her. The prospect of being shot at wasn't a pleasant one in any situation. "I have another idea," I said.

"What's that? If it's dangerous and illegal, you know me. I'd be happy to join in."

"It's neither," I said. "Get in the Jeep."

She did as I asked, and I did the same thing. I backed out of Crusty's driveway, but instead of taking off, I parked near the pile of brush in the road, which was clearly in the street and not in his yard.

"What are you doing?" Grace asked me as I popped out of my seat.

"I'm looking for anything scratchy," I said.

I started riffling through the pile, and soon she joined me.

We weren't interrupted, but not for long.

"What do you think you are doing?" Crusty asked in anger as he stepped out onto his porch. To my horror, he did indeed have a rifle in his hands.

At least he wasn't pointing it in our direction.

Yet.

"This isn't your land," I said.

"No, but I told you to go, and that's exactly what you need to do."

"Come on, Suzanne," Grace said behind me.

"Fine," I said, standing in place for a moment to give Crusty a solemn stare before I got back in and drove off. I was biting my lip as I headed down the road, but to my surprise, Grace giggled.

"What's so funny?" I asked her.

In reply, she held up a short section of branch, full of prickly leaves that were quickly losing their luster. "I found this buried under the pile."

"So, he was telling the truth," I said.

"Maybe. Then again, what if he scratched his arm at the pie shop, and *that's* when he decided to do a little pruning? It's the perfect cover, don't you think?"

"It's absolutely brilliant, if it's true," I said. "The real question is if Crusty is smart enough to think of it."

"I can't say that he isn't," Grace replied.

"That's not exactly a firm answer, but he has to stay near the top of our list, right beside Beatrice." I drove for a few more minutes, but when we got back to the diner, I looked at Grace and said, "Now I can't get pie off my mind. All this talk about it has gotten me hungry for dessert. Will we look like idiots going back in so soon for something we turned down earlier?"

Grace laughed. "Who cares what we look like if it means we get pie after all."

I parked, and we went inside. Trish was checking someone out, and when she was finished, she asked us with a puzzled look on her face, "Did you two forget something?"

"Is it too late to take you up on that earlier offer for pie?" I asked her.

"No, ma'am, it's always time for dessert," she said. She frowned for a moment before adding, "I'm glad you want pie, because I just sold the last piece of orange pineapple cake. I can't keep that stuff around."

"I'm perfectly happy with a slice of pie. Cherry sounds delightful, if you've got it," I said.

"Would you mind adding some ice cream, too?" Grace asked.

"Is there any other way to eat pie?" Trish asked her with a smile.

Grace shrugged. "Not in my book."

Trish lingered for a moment, and then she asked us, "Listen, are you two busy with anything that you don't want anyone overhearing, or can I join you?"

"By all means, make it three," I said. What Grace and I would lose in alone time would more than be made up for in time spent with a dear friend of ours. After all, we couldn't eat, breathe, and sleep murder, anyway. If nothing else, it was bad for the digestion.

As Grace and I settled at a table near the front, I saw that she was frowning. "Suzanne, this bandage thing is really bothering me," she said.

"What do you mean?"

"I still think there's a chance we're making a mountain out of a molehill. You went through those bushes yourself, and I can't see *any* signs of marks on your arms now."

I studied them both closely, and though I could still see a few faint traces of the scratches that had been there earlier, they were mostly gone now. "Then again, I didn't have to spend any time freeing that door up. It's hard to tell how unruly those bushes were before I discovered them."

"True, but still," she said as she pointed to Trish. "She's got a bandage on her arm, too. Does that make *Trish* a suspect in your mind?"

"Of course not," I said as Trish noticed us looking at her

152

and joined us. "Can I get you ladies anything else? Gladys is warming the pie up for us even as we speak."

"Trish, what did you do to your arm?" I asked her as nonchalantly as I could manage. I didn't suspect her of murder, but I was curious about it now that Grace had pointed it out to me.

"This?" she asked as she held up her arm. "I scraped it on the edge of my door at home. A little piece of a nail was sticking out from the frame, and I must have brushed against it on my way in or out. It stung like a beast, and when I got inside the house, I was bleeding at a pretty good clip. Don't worry, a little Neosporin and a Band-Aid was all that it took, and I was as good as new," she said with a grin. "I took care of that nail and showed it who was boss, too. I drove that poor thing so far into the wood it will *never* come out again. It left quite a dimple in the doorframe, though."

"Sometimes you have to show these things who the boss is," Grace said with a smile. "Tell Gladys that meal was wonderful."

"Thank you," Trish said, and then she quickly amended it to add, "I will."

"Trish, how much did *you* have to do with tonight's special?" I asked her.

"Me? I just supervise around here," she replied with a smile.

"*Trish,*" I pushed. "The truth."

"Suzanne, *everybody* needs a helping hand now and then. The poor woman is off her game, so I stepped in and helped out a little. You would have done the same thing if it had been Emma," she said, almost accusing me of being good-natured.

"You bet I would have," I said with a smile. "You've got a good heart, ma'am."

In a low voice, she said, "Thanks. Just don't spread it around, okay?"

"You bet."

As expected, the pie and ice cream were outstanding. I probably didn't need the calories, but wow, was it delicious. The company was even better, though.

As we were leaving the diner, Trish said, "I'm sure that I'll see you ladies tomorrow. In the meantime, try to stay out of trouble, would you?"

"We could try, but what fun would that be?" Grace asked her with a laugh.

"I know, but do it anyway," she said.

"We'll do our best, but we can't make any promises," I said as I touched her shoulder lightly. "Watch out for those nails now, you hear?"

"The nails need to watch out for me," she answered happily, and I knew that she was right. Trish wielding a hammer was a very frightening prospect indeed, especially if you happened to be a protruding nail head.

I half expected to find someone else lurking outside of the Boxcar Grill when Grace and I emerged from the diner, but if anyone was there, they were better at playing Hide and Go Seek than I was.

As I drove us both back toward home, I had a sudden thought. "I've got a little time before I have to go to bed," I said. "Are you up for a visit?"

"You know me, I'm always ready for anything. Who exactly are we going to go see?"

"I thought we might pop in on Gabby and Leanne. I'm curious to see what they say about Beatrice's wild accusations."

"That sounds like it could be useful," she said. "Besides, maybe Gabby won't kill us if there are two of us."

"Maybe, but I wouldn't count on it." I was only half kidding at the time. I wasn't all that excited about bracing the woman in her own home again, but I needed to be certain that Beatrice had really been making up everything she'd said to us earlier at the diner, and there was only one solid way to find out.

I had to ask her myself.

CHAPTER 16

"Hey, Gabby. I'm sorry to bother you, but I was wondering if Grace and I could come in for a minute."

She just shrugged as she stepped aside out of the threshold. "You might as well. This seems to be our night for visitors."

"Who else is here?" I asked as we walked back into the stylish home for the second time in two days.

"Jane Preston is also visiting," Gabby said.

That completely caught me off guard. What was my former schoolteacher doing at Gabby's house? While it was true that we hadn't completely eliminated her as a suspect, she had certainly shifted to the lower end of the list. "Cool," I said.

"You might as well come into the living room," Gabby said. Clearly feeling a little uncomfortable playing hostess, she asked, "Would you ladies like some sweet tea?"

Grace looked at me, but I shook my head. Not only did I not want to load my system with any more caffeine than was already in it, but I also wasn't crazy on pressing Gabby's hospitality. "We're fine," I said, "but thanks, anyway."

Gabby looked at me, puzzled for a moment. "Suzanne Hart, don't you think I know how to make good sweet tea? That's the second time I've offered it to you in the past few days, and it is also the second time you've refused it."

Oh, no. Had I offended the Southern woman in her somehow? "I just didn't want you to go to any trouble, that's all."

"It's no trouble at all. I'll make it two," she said to Grace, who simply nodded.

Leanne saved us from any further embarrassment by calling out to us, "Ladies, come on in. What brings you out so late? Suzanne, isn't it past your bedtime?" she asked with a weak grin. Maybe she was getting some of her spirit back, which would be a very good thing, given the circumstances.

"Not quite yet," I said. "Hello, Mrs. Preston. I wasn't expecting to find you here."

"It was spur of the moment," my former teacher said with a cryptic smile. Had we just interrupted something? I wasn't exactly sure. "You just missed the police chief."

That certainly got Grace's attention. "What was Chief Grant doing here?" she asked.

"He wanted to follow up on the poison that was used to kill Maggie," Gabby said as she walked in with two large glasses of sweet tea. There was no way I was going to get to sleep tonight if I drank even a third of that, but it was better than offending Gabby more than I already had.

"What did he have to say?" I asked as I took a sip of the concoction. If anything, it was even sweeter than mine, which was saying something, but I managed a hearty swallow anyway, since Gabby was watching me closely. "Ummm. That's delightful," I said with a smile.

Grace did the same thing, and that seemed to satisfy our hostess.

"You were saying?" I asked Leanne and Mrs. Preston, but Gabby answered for them. Though I had called her Jane a few times earlier, I still couldn't do it on a regular basis, even in my own mind. "The concentrated chemical used is present just about everywhere. There's some of the cleaner at the pie shop, but that's not really all that alarming. I have some of the same stuff in question here, and I wager you have it at the donut shop and at home too, Suzanne."

"That's probably true, but I don't have any idea how to reduce it down to where it would be lethal enough to use to coat pills."

"Actually, it's not that hard to find on the Internet," Mrs. Preston said.

I looked at her oddly. "Are you saying that you actually looked it up?"

"Didn't you? I was naturally curious about it," Mrs. Preston said. "I just figured *everyone* would search for it."

"That's true. I did myself," Leanne admitted softly.

"As did I," Grace added.

"You *did*?" I asked her. Why hadn't she told me she'd done that?

"I meant to say something to you this afternoon, but we've both been kind of distracted today," Grace replied, clearly trying to apologize to me for the slip-up.

"That's perfectly understandable," I said, offering her a smile to show that it wasn't going to be an issue between us. "Opportunity and means might be pretty universal with that side door secret passageway and with that cleaner being so ubiquitous, but that still leaves a big hole when it comes to motive, and as far as I'm concerned, that's the most crucial part of the case."

"Speaking of motive, you should hear what Beatrice Branch has to say about all of you," Grace said.

I hadn't been all that sure that we should mention what we'd heard to anyone else yet after what we'd just learned, but that ship had most certainly sailed now. Then again, Grace's instincts were usually dead on when it came to things like that, so I wasn't even upset that she had said something. After all, that pot needed to be stirred every chance we got.

"What exactly did she say about me?" Gabby asked, clearly unamused by the prospect of being mentioned for consideration as a possible killer.

I took another sip of tea to fortify myself before I told her. "She said that Maggie did something to offend you, and that the only reason you've been helping us solve the case is because you're trying to keep us from learning the truth."

I wasn't at all sure how Gabby was going to take it, so her laughter was a welcome relief. "If being irritated with people was truly grounds for murder, half this town would be dead."

I just shook my head, aware yet again that people continued to surprise me. Gabby composed herself after a moment as she said, "Tell us her other fanciful notions."

"Let's see. She said that Crusty probably stole money from Maggie, and so he must have killed her to keep her from turning him in to the police," I reported.

"What money would he even be able to steal?" Leanne asked. "I already told you that she didn't have two nickels to rub together."

"Something I can vouch for as well," Gabby said. "Did you think to challenge Beatrice about any of this nonsense, or did you just let her stand there and slander us without consequence?" She was angry now, but then again, I'd been fully expecting that in the first place, so I wasn't all that surprised.

"As a matter of fact, we were all sitting down at the time," Grace said.

It was not a great time for Grace to try to be amusing. "We told her what Leanne had mentioned to us earlier."

"And how did she react to that?" Leanne asked.

"She moved on to her next suspect. After Crusty, she went after Gabby, and then you, Mrs. Preston," I said, looking at my schoolteacher.

She looked at me first and then at Grace, clearly not at all certain how much information my mother had shared with us about her true relationship with Crusty. I tried to give her my most reassuring look as I said, "She thought you were vying with Maggie for Crusty's affections," I said, doing my best to make light of it.

"I don't know why people keep mentioning that," Mrs. Preston said. "The man is repugnant to me on so many levels."

"I have found that people are generally idiots," Gabby said, her composure regained once again. I didn't share her belief about that, but I didn't feel that it made much sense to get into a debate about it.

"What did she say about me?" Leanne asked, her voice soft and vulnerable.

"She mentioned a few things that we'd already discussed with you," I said, trying to spare her the embarrassment of rehashing the rumors we'd heard about her.

"That makes the least amount of sense of all," Gabby said. "Leanne was around Maggie nearly twenty-four hours a day. She wouldn't need a secret passageway to get in to poison her."

"Not that I would do it anyway," Leanne said. "The truth is that I'm lost without Maggie."

"I told you not to worry about it," Gabby said as she patted Leanne's shoulder. As she did so, she shot me a deadly look, and then she shifted it to Grace for a moment before dropping it. "Thank you for stopping by, but I'm sure you need to get home so you can get some rest, Suzanne. After all, you'll be up before long so you can make your donuts again. I don't know how you do it."

"It's not work if you love doing it," I said, but I wasn't about to be ushered out so quickly. "Mrs. Preston, I was surprised to find you here."

"I called her," Leanne said sheepishly.

"Really? I didn't realize that," Gabby said. It appeared that it was a night full of secrets.

"I just wanted to get some advice from her," Leanne said.

"What possible advice could a retired schoolteacher have for you that you couldn't get elsewhere, and closer to home?" Gabby asked, clearly miffed that she wasn't the be all and end all for her houseguest, and family member to boot.

"It's all perfectly innocent," Mrs. Preston said. "I mentioned to her that I'd served some time in the school guidance counselor's office, and she said that she might be interested in a career change now that Maggie was gone."

It sounded innocent enough to me, but Gabby certainly didn't take it that way. "You are a pie maker, young lady."

"Sure, but that doesn't mean that it's the *only* thing I can do," Leanne protested, rather weakly, though.

"We'll discuss it later when we're alone again," Gabby said. This time when she turned to Grace and me, the opportunity to extend our stay was clearly over.

"Gabby's right," I said as I stood and put my nearly empty glass on the provided coaster. "I need my sleep if I'm going to be worth anything tomorrow. Good night, ladies."

As Grace and I started to leave, Mrs. Preston piped up, "I'll join you. Thanks again for the tea."

"Certainly," Gabby said icily. Clearly she was unhappy that Leanne had gone to her, and there might be a chill in the air between the two women for quite some time.

At least she wasn't upset with me.

Once we were outside, I turned to Mrs. Preston. "What do you think is going to happen with Leanne?"

"Gabby will find a way to tie her to that pie shop, one way or the other," she replied. "I'm not saying it's the worst thing in the world for her. I just thought she should consider her options before committing to anything now that Maggie is gone."

"That was sweet of you," Grace said, but there wasn't a great deal of warmth in her voice.

Our former teacher looked surprised by the inflection behind the comment. "I help wherever and whenever I have the opportunity. I always have, and I always will."

After our former teacher walked away, Grace and I got back into my Jeep and took the short drive back toward our respective homes. "Were you implying something back there with Mrs. Preston?" I asked her.

"I don't know. It just seemed a little odd finding her there tonight. One might almost say it was all a little *too* convenient."

"In what way?" I asked, clearly puzzled by Grace's reaction. "Don't you believe her?"

"Most of me does, but let's say for one moment that she was the killer, and we've missed something. She might have come by Gabby's to see if she could get some information out of her."

"But *Leanne* called her, remember?" I asked.

"Yes, but there are ways of getting yourself invited places that sound as though it wasn't your idea in the first place. I shouldn't have to tell *you* that, Suzanne."

"Hey, Sally Jackson *meant* to invite me to that pool party in high school. It just must have slipped her mind," I said, knowing full well what Grace was referring to.

"Well, showing up in your swimsuit certainly reminded her," Grace said with a hint of laughter in her voice. "Forget I said anything. I'm sure I'm just being paranoid."

"I'm not knocking you for it," I said. "Being paranoid is the only thing that has kept us alive a few times in the past."

"And may it serve as well many times in the future," Grace

said as I pulled into her driveway. "So, where do things stand at the moment with our investigation?"

I gave myself a few moments to ponder before answering. "My gut is telling me that it was either Crusty or Beatrice. I'm not saying that no one else could have done it, but they both just feel tainted by this in my mind." I thought about mentioning what I'd seen in Beatrice's purse earlier, or at least what I thought I'd seen, but I couldn't figure out how to bring it up without sounding completely paranoid, something that Grace was already overly sensitive about.

"I know what you mean," Grace said. "The three ladies we spoke with tonight are less likely suspects in my mind too, but by this point we are usually able to narrow things down quite a bit more than we can now."

"The problem is that too many people had the motive, means, and opportunity to kill Maggie," I said. "The truth of the matter is that I'm not quite sure *how* we're going to break this case. Maybe we need to stir the pot even more than we already have."

"I don't see how we can do that, short of accusing everyone we suspect of the murder, and see who reacts the most violently."

"Yes, maybe that's not the best game plan after all," I said. "Tell you what. Let's both sleep on it and see where we are tomorrow after I close Donut Hearts for the day. Are you free again?"

"As long as you need me," she said. After a moment, Grace added, "You know, you could always stay here with me tonight if you don't want to be at the cottage alone."

"Thanks, but I'm so beat I suspect that I'll be asleep before my head hits the pillow."

"Even with all of that sweet tea in you? Between the caffeine and the sugar, I'll be bouncing off the walls all night."

"I can't afford to stay awake," I admitted. "I'm going home

and going to bed. Shoot, I might not even stop long enough to change into my pajamas."

"Please do that at least," Grace said with a smile.

"Good night, Grace," I said.

"Good night, Suzanne. Sweet dreams."

"Right back at you," I said.

I started to turn on the lights in the cottage when I got there, but something stayed my hand. I had heard a rustling in the bushes outside my door when I'd gotten home, or at least I thought I had. Was someone out there? Could the murderer have grown tired of my incessant questions and decided to do something to shut me up once and for all? The old me might have gone outside with a baseball bat to confront whoever might be lurking outside, but I'd been through too many situations where such behavior had nearly been the end of me.

So I did the only sensible thing I could think of.

I called the police.

CHAPTER 17

I HAD TO GIVE STEPHEN GRANT credit. Within two minutes, he had not only gotten to my place, but he was outside with a flashlight looking around the cottage with two other officers. I'd started to open the door to join them when he'd motioned for me to stay right where I was.

After ten minutes, his two officers got back into their squad car and drove away while Stephen climbed my porch steps.

That was clearly my cue to join him.

"Did you see anything?" I asked him anxiously.

"No, nothing out of the ordinary," he replied.

"I'm sorry I wasted your time," I apologized. "I know you have better things to do than to chase down my imaginary visitors in the middle of the night."

Chief Grant shook his head. "That's not the way that I see it. Suzanne, you did *exactly* the right thing. Just because we didn't find anything doesn't mean that someone wasn't out there. When there is a killer on the loose, I'd rather you be safe than sorry."

"I guess I do have a reason to be a little jumpy," I said as I yawned. "Anyway, thanks for coming out. It was probably nothing more than a raccoon looking for food."

"Just in case it wasn't, though, I'll have either Darby or Rick patrol your way every fifteen or twenty minutes for the rest of the night."

"That's not necessary," I said, suddenly feeling very

foolish about jumping at shadows, no matter if there might be justification to see boogey men wherever I looked or not.

"Maybe not, but it's happening anyway." He grinned at me as he added, "Besides, if anything happened to you while Jake was away, your husband would have my hide."

"Yes, Jake has a habit of being overprotective when it comes to me," I said. "Listen, I've tried not to butt into your personal life, but you need to give Grace another chance."

The chief of police shook his head as he rubbed his chin. "Suzanne, she didn't do anything wrong. It's all me."

"Don't you think I know that?" I asked him sternly.

"Wow, that was kind of harsh."

"Maybe that's what you need right now, Stephen. She loves you, and I know you love her, too. So what if you have an important job that takes up a lot of your time? Grace isn't a child. She can live with that. What she can't live with is your inability to show her how much you care about her. That is something totally within your power to change, and if you don't, you're going to regret it for the rest of your life, because you are never going to find a woman as good as the one you're about to lose from sheer stupidity on your part."

The chief of police took my words like body blows, and I felt a little bad for beating him up so badly, especially when he'd made it a point to come to my rescue so quickly, but the words needed to be said, and if I lost him as a friend, it was a price I was willing to risk.

"Yeah," he finally said, after looking as though he wanted to cry. "I've been thinking the same thing. I just don't know how to fix things. They've kind of gotten out of hand at this point. I really messed up. I do love her, you know."

"Then go tell her, you idiot!" I said, smacking the chief of police on the forehead. Ordinarily I wouldn't advise that kind of behavior toward an officer of the law, but if anyone deserved a good clout, it was Stephen Grant, whether he was our chief of police or the president of the United States. "It's not too late right now, but it might be tomorrow."

"I'll wake her up if I go there this late," he said, grasping at one last excuse not to do what we both knew was right.

"Even if that were true, I've got a hunch she won't be too upset after she hears what you've got to say for yourself. Besides, you know Grace. She's probably still up. Now be a man and go tell her how you feel. That's an order."

Chief Grant finally managed the ghost of a grin. "Okay. Thanks. I guess I needed that."

"It was my pleasure. Now go!"

He saluted me as his smile broadened. "Yes, ma'am."

I didn't think I'd be able to go to sleep after all that excitement, but exhaustion is the best sleeping pill there is, at least as far as I was concerned. Before I knew it, my alarm was giving its shrill call, and it was time to get up and go to work, despite what might be happening in the world around me. I got dressed, grabbed a quick bite to eat for breakfast, and then I walked out my door, only to find another car in my driveway.

There was no cause for alarm, though.

It was a police cruiser, and Darby Jones was leaning against the driver's-side door, clearly waiting for me.

"What are *you* doing here?" I asked him as I walked toward the police officer.

"I've got orders to give you a police escort to your place of work," he said in an official manner.

"That's completely unnecessary," I said, though I felt a little relieved having him there all the same. "Have you been here all night?"

"No, but Rick and I have been taking turns checking up on you. You'll be happy to know that we believe we've found your culprit."

"Really? Did you arrest someone?" Could the case really be over that easily?

"No, I didn't want to take a wild animal into custody. I gave him a stern warning to keep away from your place, though," Darby said with a grin.

"Was it a raccoon after all?"

"No, but a skunk is even worse," he said.

"And you actually confronted him? You're a brave man," I answered with a grin.

"Hey, we serve and protect around here. Are you ready for your escort?"

"You're not going to use your siren and lights, are you?"

Darby shook his head. "No, that might be pushing it. Is that okay with you if we skip that part?"

"I suppose so," I said, pretending to be disappointed. After all, it was three o'clock in the morning. I doubted anyone would welcome a show at that hour.

As I drove by Grace's place, the lights were out, and there was only one car, hers, in her driveway. I wondered how that particular conversation had gone with the police chief, but I knew that I wouldn't have to wonder long. Grace would tell me all about it in eight hours when she came by the shop so we could start sleuthing again.

Darby pulled in right beside me when I got out of my Jeep.

"You've done your duty, Officer. There's no need to see me to the door."

"I'm just following orders, ma'am," he said with a grin. "Do you mind if I have a look around inside first?"

"No, that's fine," I said, though I thought it was unnecessary.

The front door lock looked to be intact, and I knew that getting in through the back way would take a tank, that door was so thick and heavily bolted. After I unlocked the front door and flipped on a few lights, Darby motioned me to go back outside, but I pointed to a nearby couch and sat in front instead. After all, I knew that I'd be safer there than I would have been standing around outside waiting for him to finish his search. Darby shrugged as he disappeared into the kitchen, and three minutes later he was back. It wasn't that big a space to investigate, after all.

"All clear," he said.

"Sorry I can't offer you any coffee, but if you come by later, you can have a cup, and a fresh cake donut, too."

"I might just take you up on that," he said. "But for now, I have to get back out there."

"Thanks again," I said as I unlocked the door to let him out.

"Thank the chief," Darby said. "It was all his idea, not that I minded. See you later, Suzanne."

"Bye," I said.

After the door was safely locked behind him, I got to work. When times were crazy in my life, for whatever reason, I found great solace in the routine of making donuts. There was something calming and tranquil about the experience as I got lost in the patterns I repeated nearly every day of my adult life.

Those patterns were interrupted, however, when my cell phone rang.

There was only one person who could be sure that I was awake at this hour, and I was dying to speak with him.

"Jake! What are you still doing up?" I asked him, laughing as I said it. "I miss you, you big goof."

169

"Well, you won't have to for much longer," he said, matching my tone of joy. "This time tomorrow, I'll be back in April Springs where I belong."

"You're not quitting the case, are you?" I asked him. "If you are, I hope you're not doing it because of me." I knew that no matter how hard he'd been working lately, Jake had been thriving by getting back to some kind of work, an opportunity to feel as though he was useful again. He'd missed it in his short retirement, and I doubted that he even realized how much until he'd gotten back into a routine that was all his own.

"We cracked it, Suzanne," he said with a laugh. "At first, I thought Mr. Armitage was crazy hiring us and keeping us on his payroll, but a few things started to fall together, and we caught a lucky break. One of his former employees was planning to do some very bad things, but we stopped him just in time. The man had enough weapons in his trunk to supply a small army, and he was getting ready to use them when we caught him."

"Was anyone hurt?" I asked.

"Well, his ego was a little bruised because we caught him before he could do anything," Jake said, "but that was it. He's in police custody now, and we all just got bonuses for a job well done. Suzanne, I know that lottery money is just about gone, but you won't have to worry about making ends meet for quite a while. Our boss was *very* generous."

"Why wouldn't he be? After all, you saved his life," I said, proud of my husband yet again.

"Well, it wasn't *just* me. We had a pretty strong team."

"Fine, you're *all* great guys," I said. "When exactly are you coming back?" I wanted to ask him to come home straight away, but I knew I couldn't do that.

"That's the thing. I've been up thirty-six hours straight, and I'm in pretty bad need of some sleep. First thing in the morning we're all giving statements to the local police and the FBI, but I should be home in time for dinner tomorrow night. Let's go out and celebrate. How about Napoli's?" he asked me.

"I'd love to, but I'm afraid they're closed," I said.

"For good?" he asked, the heartbreak clear in his voice.

"No, the ladies are taking a two-week vacation to Italy. In fact, they are probably in the air even as we speak."

"Good for them. We could use another vacation ourselves, and now we have enough money to do it right. What do you say?"

I wanted to tell him about Maggie's murder and my investigation with Grace, but I couldn't bring myself to bring down our happy conversation. "We can talk about it when you get back. I can't wait to see you, Jake."

"Not half as much as I want to see you," he said. "If I haven't told you enough lately, I love you, Suzanne, and I'm awfully glad you came into my life."

"I couldn't agree with you more," I said, feeling the warm glow of his love even through the phone. "Now get some sleep, young man. You have a lot to do in the next fifteen hours."

"I can't wait," he said.

After Jake was off the line, I began to feel guilty about not telling him about Maggie's murder. He deserved to know, but it wasn't as though I was purposely keeping anything from him. There had just never been a good time to bring it up. When he got back into town, after we had our sweet reunion, there would be plenty of time to catch him up to speed on what had been happening in his absence.

In the meantime, I still had donuts to make, and now I was behind in a very tight schedule, but it had been worth every second I'd stolen from my day.

Jake was coming home to me, and that was really all that mattered!

CHAPTER 18

I ALMOST HAD TO SKIP MY break entirely because the phone call with Jake had cut into my tight schedule, but I knew that if I didn't spend at least a few minutes outside, the day would seem unbearably long. For the second time in a very short day, I went outside to find someone waiting for me, but it wasn't Darby, or even the police chief this time.

Leanne Haller was sitting on a chair at my outdoor table, and from the look of it, she'd been crying for quite some time.

I took the seat across from her and reached out and touched her hand. "Leanne, are you okay?"

"Suzanne, I just don't know what to do. I need some advice." She dabbed at her cheeks and wiped away a few of the tears, but from the tone in her voice, I knew more were surely to follow.

"I'm sorry, but I can't help you with career choices, but Mrs. Preston is probably pretty good at it," I replied as I slid my coffee cup across the table to her. "I haven't had any yet, so you're welcome to this."

"Thanks, but if I drink that, I'll *never* get to sleep. Jane is fine and all, and so is Gabby, but you're the only one who knows what it's like to put your heart and soul into something you make with your very own hands. How can I give that up?"

"You don't have to," I said. "You said yourself that a lot of folks have offered to help you. For that matter, I'd be glad to do whatever I can to make opening the pie shop a reality."

"But in the end, it all falls on my shoulders. How do you manage to do it year after year?"

I could tell this young woman an idealized version of my real life, but I felt as though I owed her the stark realities of running a small business alone. "I won't lie to you. It's not easy," I said. "You have to want it from the bottom of your heart, and then you have to make it your single purpose in life, especially at first. I once heard someone say that people who work for themselves would rather put in eighty hours a week than work for someone else for forty, and I've found that to be true, especially when you're just starting out."

She looked suitably depressed. "Are you sorry that you did it?"

"Me? No, it's not only what I do, it's become who I *am*," I said. "It also brought my husband into my life in a roundabout way, so I'd be grateful for that if nothing else. But I don't want to lie to you. It's hard, even without the handicap you're going to be starting out with. Until Maggie's murder is solved, it will be hanging over your head like a grand piano, just waiting to fall."

"You and Grace are still working on the case, though, aren't you?" she asked me, tentatively reaching out to take the offered coffee.

"As a matter of fact, things are coming quickly to a head. We've got it narrowed down to two of our top suspects, and I'm pretty sure I knew who it was that killed her. It was pretty clever actually, rigging that door up the way they did."

The truth was, I thought Beatrice had found a way to get inside the pie shop when no one else was there, and she'd rigged the door to get in and out easily. After all, she'd had a set of plans in her bag at the diner. Maybe she'd found a way to get her hands on the blueprints of the shop. How else would she know about the door? If only I'd had the nerve and the brains to snatch them out of her purse when I'd first seen them.

"So then, you know," she said softly.

"I think so," I said. "I need to check a few things out this afternoon, but it might all be over in twelve hours."

Leanne nodded, clearly taken aback by my statement. "You don't have any donuts in there, do you? I'll even take something stale if you've got it."

"I have some freshly made cake donuts," I told her. "How does that sound?"

"Like perfection," she said.

"Then let's get you something to eat."

Once we were safely locked inside, I led Leanne back into the kitchen. "There's fresh coffee out front if you need to refresh yours, and I think I'll join you. What looks good to you?" I asked her as I surveyed the donuts I'd just finished.

"I think this will do nicely," Leanne said as she reached over and picked up the heavy batter dropper I used to make my cake donuts. Though I'd rinsed it in the sink, there were still remnants of the last batter I'd dropped into the hot oil clinging to the sides of it.

"I'm all out of batter," I said, confused by what she was doing at first, but then I got it. "Leanne, do me a favor and put that back where it was."

"Suzanne, I'm sorry, but I don't see any other way out of this mess for me. Clearly you know I killed my aunt, and if there's any chance for me to ever open that pie shop, you can't be around to tell the police what you know."

174

It was Leanne? I had been wrong about her, but the puzzle pieces started rearranging themselves in my mind in the split second I realized that she was indeed the killer. I'd suspected her at first, but her story had been so convincing that she wasn't resentful about the cookbook, or the partnership that was never offered her! What a fool I'd been. I'd taken her love of creating goodies in the kitchen, and I had assumed that someone who loved to bake so much couldn't possibly be a coldblooded killer! It galled me knowing that Beatrice had been right about at least one thing the night before!

"Leanne, it's never too late to do the right thing. Don't do anything you're going to regret," I said as I looked for something to use to fight back with. Unfortunately, the knives were either in drawers or in the sink, which was where Leanne was standing. The oil was hot, but I was closer to it than she was, so anything I threw in there would likely burn me a great deal more than it would her.

"I'm afraid you're wrong about that," she said, biting her lower lip as she swung the dropper at my head, trying to decapitate me with it without any warning at all.

I did the only thing I could do, which was to try to block her blow.

It worked, at least partially, as I put my arm up to stop the weight from crashing down on my skull.

It broke my arm in the process, though.

I could feel the bone snap upon impact, and wave after wave of pain washed through me. My right arm hung lifelessly down by my side, and I hurt so badly that I could barely see through the agony. "Don't hit me again!" I cried out as I crumpled to the floor, cradling my dead arm in my lap.

"If you'd just stay right where you are, it will be over in a second," Leanne said as though she were scolding a misbehaving child.

I wasn't about to do that, though.

My arm might be dead, but there was nothing wrong with my feet. Lashing out with both of them from my sitting position, I brought her down with a thud.

As I lay there trying to overcome the wash of agony I felt from any movement at all, I kept waiting for her to jump up and hit me one last, deadly time.

She didn't move, though.

After a few moments trying to catch enough breath to withstand what I knew was going to be sheer torture, I managed to crawl over to Leanne.

A pool of blood continued to spread out from the back of her head. I searched for a pulse with my good hand, but there was nothing there, not even a flutter.

I tried my best to get my cell phone out of my pocket to call for help, but I must have passed out from the pain my attempts had brought on.

When I came to again, I tried once more, finally managing to worm my cell phone out of my pocket and dying a little inside with each slight movement.

I finally got it free of my pocket only to realize that the fall had damaged it beyond repair.

I could stay right where I was until someone got suspicious and broke into the donut shop to find me, or I could somehow crawl out to the door where I could be more easily seen.

There was no way I could stay with that slowly cooling corpse, one that I had caused myself, even if it had been done in self-defense.

I couldn't allow myself to think about that, though.

I had to take care of myself first.

Slowly, trying not to jar my arm too much but failing miserably with each push, I worked my way out of the kitchen and into the dining room, sliding on my side as I went. I'd tried to stand a few times, but there was no way I could manage it without passing out again, and if I did anything, I had to stay awake.

The only problem was that I was still behind the counter even after I got out of the kitchen. No one could see me from the outside from where I was at the moment.

And then I heard a tap on the front door.

"I'm here," I said as loudly as I could, trying to shout despite the pain that raced through my body with every breath. "Help."

I must not have gotten enough volume out of my voice, though, because the tap quickly went away.

It looked as though I was going to be there for a very long time after all.

CHAPTER 19

S UDDENLY, IT SOUNDED AS THOUGH the entire front window of my shop exploded, sending glass shards flying everywhere.

I was glad that I had the counter for protection.

"Suzanne? Are you all right?" Darby asked as he rushed in and knelt beside my body.

"My arm is broken pretty badly," I said. Almost as an afterthought, I added, "Leanne is dead. I killed her. She's back there." I couldn't even risk pointing, the pain was so bad.

And then I passed out again.

When I woke up, I was in the hospital. My mind felt fuzzy, and there was an odd taste of cotton in my mouth. I looked down at my broken arm and realized that there was just a dull throbbing pain there now where so recently it had nearly ruined me.

"You're going to be okay, Suzanne," Momma said as her face hovered into view.

That was all that I heard as I quickly faded away again. I wasn't sure what kind of painkillers I was on, but I knew they were the strongest things I'd ever experienced in my life.

The next time I woke up, Jake was there. "You made it back," I said groggily. "Are you okay?"

"I'm fine," he said as he stroked my hair, saw me wince, and then he pulled his hand back immediately. "I'm so sorry I wasn't here for you."

"Not your fault," I whispered. "She rigged the door herself to make it look like someone else did it, didn't she?" I'd had nightmares envisioning Leanne setting the stage to create other suspects in her aunt's murder, and I didn't even need Jake's assurance to know that I was right.

"We'll talk about it later, honey," he said.

"Is she dead? Don't answer that. She is. I know it."

Jake knew better than to lie to me. "Suzanne, it was either her or you. I'm perfectly happy with the choice you made."

"Me, too," I said, and then I fell asleep again.

CHAPTER 20

C HIEF GRANT WAS WITH JAKE the next time I woke up. "If you're up to it, Jake thought you'd like to know what we've found out," he said.

"I want to know," I said as I struggled to sit up. It caused another wave of deadening pain, and I suspected my medication had worn off.

"I'll go get your doctor," Jake said as he started for the door.

"No!" I said as loudly as I could manage. "Whatever they are giving me is making my brain fuzzy. I need to hear this. Please."

He agreed, but I could see that doing so caused him some very real pain as well.

"We found evidence of the poison hidden in her apartment," the chief said. "She threw away the pan she used, but it was still in the trash can. Kind of a rookie mistake, that."

"I still can't figure out why she poisoned only half the pills. Why not one, or even all of them?"

"Who knows? It may have been all of the concentrated solution she had, and she didn't want any of it to go to waste."

I suppose that made sense in a skewed kind of way. "What about the side door?" I asked.

"It was all in her journal, if you can imagine that. Who writes these things down?"

"Teenage girls," I said, and then I coughed a bit, sending another wave of pain through my body, but particularly into my arm. "Some women never lose the habit," I added after my coughing fit subsided. "What else did it say?"

"She found the door by accident, and she'd already decided to kill Maggie. It wasn't over the pie shop, though. She went into great detail about how Maggie had found her notes on a book she was going to publish herself and then she stole them from her. When Leanne confronted her about it, Maggie laughed it off and told her to grow up, this was the real world. That's when she decided to kill her. We searched her Internet browsing history, and Leanne had indeed looked up the easiest way to poison someone."

"She admitted doing that last night out of a sense of morbid curiosity about the poisoning," I said, remembering her confession of sorts.

"Sure, but we were able to determine that she did it *before* the murder, not after," the chief said. "What else is there? Oh, yes. The scratches on her arms were from the bushes, not the oven like she told you and Grace. Am I missing anything?"

"Beatrice had something in her purse when I saw her at the diner. It looked like blueprints or something. Were they of the pie shop?"

"Oh, she mentioned that when I interviewed her about the case," the chief said. "She's thinking about putting in a gazebo in her backyard, and she even showed me the plans she'd found for one online. She said if she was planning to kill someone, would she be building a gazebo? Whatever that was supposed to mean."

So, I'd jumped to the wrong conclusion about that altogether. This case wasn't my brightest moment as an amateur sleuth, and I was beginning to wonder if this might not be the perfect time to quit. After all, it had nearly cost me my life. If I hadn't managed to block that blow, I would be dead now, and nothing else would really matter.

"Suzanne? May I please call the doctor now?" Jake asked, imploring me to let him summon help.

"Yes, please," I said meekly.

"Anyway, I just thought you ought to know," the chief said. "Take care."

"How are you and Grace doing?" I managed to ask as they gave me more medication.

"We're going to be just fine, thanks to you. She and your mother are in the cafeteria rounding up some coffee," he said. "I'd hug you, but it might hurt."

"Love sometimes does that," I said, and then I was out again.

CHAPTER 21

"How's your arm?" Jake asked me two weeks later as we drove toward the mountains, and away from April Springs.

"It's better, but it still hurts quite a bit," I said.

"Don't worry, it will heal, given time." It was the voice of experience, but I knew that it wasn't going to be easy.

"At least Emma and Sharon are taking over Donut Hearts until further notice," I said. We'd quickly come to an agreement, and the two of them had been more than happy to step in.

"For the time being, but you'll be back at it before you know it," Jake said as he reached over and patted my leg. "In the meantime, the only thing you need to do is get better. Your mother got us this cabin for the next two months, and you don't have to worry about a thing until then."

"I might not go back ever again," I said, voicing something that had been running through my thoughts ever since the confrontation with Leanne.

"You feel that way now, but you'll change your mind," Jake said, risking a glance at me as he drove up the steady curving road.

"I wouldn't be so sure of that," I said. I could still see Leanne's lifeless body lying in my kitchen, the blood slowly spreading out from under her head onto the floor. How could I ever bring myself to go back there? Everyone had urged me to visit it at least once before we left, but I hadn't been able to bring myself to do it.

Maybe with time I'd be able to watch that memory fade into the background, but I couldn't be sure.

All I knew with any certainty at the moment was that I needed to stay as far away from April Springs, and Donut Hearts, as I could.

Only time would tell if I'd ever be able to go back.

But regardless of what the future might hold for me, I knew that I would be okay. After all, I had Jake, Momma, Grace, and an entire town full of people who loved me, and in the end, that was really all that mattered.

RECIPES

Spiced Buttermilk Donuts

There's something about buttermilk that really enhances baked goods for me. I've been using buttermilk as a substitute for regular milk occasionally for years in many of my donuts, and my entire family loves them. I don't always bother with buying fresh buttermilk, though. The powdered variety works just fine in this and any other donut recipe you might care to use it in. These donuts are best when there's a slight chill in the air, or so I think, but they are perfectly lovely any time of year!

Ingredients

- 2 eggs, beaten
- 1 cup sugar, granulated
- 1/2 stick butter, unsalted and softened
- 1 cup buttermilk
- 3 1/2 cups flour
- 2 teaspoons baking powder
- 1 teaspoon baking soda
- 1 teaspoon nutmeg
- 1 teaspoon cinnamon
- 1/4 teaspoon salt

Directions

In a large bowl, beat the eggs and then add the butter and sugar, creaming the mixture into a consistent form. Add the buttermilk, mix well, and then set this mixture aside.

In a medium bowl, sift together the flour, baking powder, baking soda, nutmeg, cinnamon, and salt.

Next, add the dry mix to the wet slowly, making sure to mix thoroughly as you go. If the mixture is too stiff, add a little more buttermilk. If it's too runny, add more flour.

Chill the dough for at least an hour, and then turn it out onto a floured surface. Knead into a ball, then roll out to approximately ½ inch thick. Cut out donuts with a cutter, and then set them aside.

Heat enough canola oil to 375 degrees F, and then drop the rounds and holes into the oil, being careful not to overcrowd them.

Fry for approximately 2 minutes per side, and then pull out of the oil and drain on a rack with paper towels below. These are good as is, or you can always add powdered sugar, icing, or even cocoa powder, if you are so inclined.

Makes approximately 1 dozen donuts and 1 dozen holes.

Donuts (Sort of) Your Kids Can Make

This recipe is a real winner with the younger crowd, but that doesn't mean that adults can't make them and enjoy them, too! It's kind of messy, so be prepared for it, but what kid doesn't like to make a mess? These are quick and easy, a winning combination on a rainy or even snowy afternoon!

Ingredients

- 1 egg
- 3/4 cup milk
- 2 teaspoons granulated sugar
- 1 cup flour, unbleached all-purpose
- 1/4 teaspoon salt
- 2 teaspoons baking powder
- Additional Ingredients
- Slices of bread, any kind (we use white)
- Jam or preserves (your favorite)
- Cinnamon sugar or icing sugar

Directions

Start heating the canola oil, enough to cover the donuts, to 375 degrees F.

In a large bowl, beat the egg and add the milk and sugar.

In another bowl, sift together the flour, salt, and baking powder, and then mix the dry ingredients into the batter.

Here's where the fun begins!

Let your kids cut the crusts off the bread, and then have them make regular jam sandwiches themselves. Cut the sandwiches into four equal pieces, dip them into the batter, and then fry them until they are golden brown.

Once they are out of the oil and cool to the touch, let your kids add their favorite toppings, from powdered sugar to cinnamon sugar to even regular icing.

Enjoy!

Yield: 8–12 squares

Cranberry Treats

I have a real affinity for cranberries, and they are great in these easy-to-make-and-serve treats. They go great with coffee or hot cocoa, but don't forget to share them with your kids! You can also use other mixes as well, and we've made blueberry treats in the past as well!

Ingredients

- 1 package cranberry muffin mix (7 ounces)
- 3⁄4 cup flour
- 1 egg, beaten
- 3⁄4 cup buttermilk
- cranberries, frozen (purely optional), then thawed.

Directions

Heat enough canola oil to 375 degrees F to fry your treats, and then get started on the batter while you wait for the oil to come up to heat.

In a medium bowl, add the extra flour to the muffin mix, combining well.

Next, add the beaten egg and the buttermilk, stirring but not overmixing this. If you decide to add extra cranberries, here is when you should do it.

It's as simple as that. Drop little balls of dough into the hot oil, frying two to three minutes per side until they are brown. Drain them directly onto paper towels.

You can eat these like this, or dust them with powdered sugar for an extra touch of sweetness.

Makes approximately 12 treats

A Different Kind of Baked Donut

I think everyone should invest in an inexpensive donut maker, but then again, I'm a bit donut crazy, and I don't care who knows it! We use portable little countertop units more these days to bake donuts than ever. We will still fry donuts on occasion, but these are so much easier, especially the cleanup, which is a real plus in my kitchen. If you don't have the space for a donut baker, though, there are donut-shaped pans you can use along with your conventional oven, as well as muffin tins in a pinch. Any way you can make yourself these baked treats is excellent as far as I'm concerned!

This particular recipe makes cake donuts denser than you might be used to, but my family loves them as a break from my usual offerings.

Ingredients

- 1 egg, beaten
- 1/2 cup sugar, white granulated
- 1/2 cup mashed potatoes
- 1/4 cup whole milk (buttermilk works great here, too)
- 4 tablespoons butter, melted
- 1 cup flour, unbleached all-purpose
- 2 teaspoons baking powder
- 1/2 teaspoon nutmeg
- 1/2 teaspoon cinnamon
- 1/4 teaspoon salt

Directions

In a large bowl, beat the egg thoroughly, and then add the sugar, mashed potatoes, milk, and melted butter. Mix thoroughly, and then set this aside.

In another bowl, sift together the flour, baking powder, nutmeg, cinnamon, and salt.

Incorporate the dry ingredients into the wet and mix together until the consistency is smooth.

Using two spoons or a cookie scoop, add portions of batter about the size of a walnut to each cavity in your baking vessel and bake 9 to 14 minutes at 360 degrees F, or until golden brown. Your method of baking may impact the cooking time, so keep an eye on them.

Once they are cool, top with powdered sugar and enjoy!

Yield: 8–12 small donuts.

If you enjoy Jessica Beck Mysteries and you would like to be notified when the next book is being released, please visit our website at jessicabeckmysteries.net for valuable information about Jessica's books, and sign up for her new-releases-only mail blast.

Your email address will not be shared, sold, bartered, traded, broadcast, or disclosed in any way. There will be no spam from us, just a friendly reminder when the latest book is being released, and of course, you can drop out at any time.

OTHER BOOKS BY JESSICA BECK

The Donut Mysteries
Glazed Murder
Fatally Frosted
Sinister Sprinkles
Evil Éclairs
Tragic Toppings
Killer Crullers
Drop Dead Chocolate
Powdered Peril
Illegally Iced
Deadly Donuts
Assault and Batter
Sweet Suspects
Deep Fried Homicide
Custard Crime
Lemon Larceny
Bad Bites
Old Fashioned Crooks
Dangerous Dough
Troubled Treats
Sugar Coated Sins
Criminal Crumbs
Vanilla Vices
Raspberry Revenge
Fugitive Filling
Devil's Food Defense
Pumpkin Pleas
Floured Felonies
Mixed Malice
Tasty Trials
Baked Books
Cranberry Crimes
Boston Cream Bribes
Cherry Filled Charges
Scary Sweets
Cocoa Crush
Pastry Penalties
Apple Stuffed Alibies
Perjury Proof

The Classic Diner Mysteries
A Chili Death
A Deadly Beef
A Killer Cake
A Baked Ham
A Bad Egg
A Real Pickle
A Burned Biscuit

The Ghost Cat Cozy Mysteries
Ghost Cat: Midnight Paws
Ghost Cat 2: Bid for Midnight

The Cast Iron Cooking Mysteries
Cast Iron Will
Cast Iron Conviction
Cast Iron Alibi
Cast Iron Motive
Cast Iron Suspicion

Made in the USA
Lexington, KY
30 March 2019